Amber leaned forward, her chin on her fists, eager to listen. Then she noticed the red button on the corner of her desk. She checked her backpack. No, her stuffed-animal-club button was still securely pinned to the flap.

It must be Mindy's button. She probably didn't realize she had lost it.

"You dropped this," Amber whispered, anxious for a chance to make up. She put the button on Mindy's desk.

Mindy pushed it back. "I didn't drop it."

"What do you mean? Don't you want it?"

Mindy whispered so Mrs. Sharp wouldn't overhear. "If you can quit third grade, Amber Cantrell, then I can quit our club."

Amber was stunned. Without Mindy, there wasn't any club. She couldn't be in a club by herself.

Feeling someone's stare, she looked up and met Delight Wakefield's eyes. Now she knew why Mindy gave back the button.

Her best friend was in Delight's club now.

Tales From Third Grade

Who Needs Third Grade?

Candice F. Ransom

Troll Associates

For Stephanie

Library of Congress Cataloging-in-Publication Data

Ransom, Candice F., (date)
   Who needs third grade? / by Candice F. Ransom.
     p.   cm.—(Tales from third grade)
   Summary: Eight-year-old Amber, still adjusting to her parents'
divorce, starts third grade and finds herself torn with jealousy
over the new girl Delight, who seems to be stealing away Amber's
best friend Mindy.
   ISBN 0-8167-2988-3 (lib. bdg.)   ISBN 0-8167-2989-1 (pbk.)
   [1. Friendship—Fiction.   2. Schools—Fiction.   3. Divorce—
Fiction.] I. Title. II. Series: Ransom, Candice F., 1952-
Tales from third grade.
PZ7.R1743Wh 1993
[Fic]—dc20   92-30754

A TROLL BOOK, published by Troll Associates.

Who Needs Third Grade?

Chapter
ONE

Amber Cantrell wasn't the least bit worried about starting third grade. She *was* worried that her father would arrive too late to take her and her best friend, Mindy Alexander, to the Labor Day carnival.

"After the next two red cars, the third red car will be Dad's," Amber said, anxiously watching the corner of Carriage and Buggy Whip.

"You said that a few minutes ago." Mindy shifted to a more comfortable position on Amber's front stoop. They'd been waiting a long time.

"I had it wrong. I said blue cars. My father has a red car. I should have said red." The charm had to be exactly right to work.

Amber craned her neck to see past her mother's rose bushes. A white truck passed, then a green mini-van, but no red cars.

"I wish he'd hurry." Closing her eyes, she impatiently willed a red car to appear.

"Ants-in-her-pants Amber" her brother Justin called her. He was in junior high, old enough to remember how Amber used to scootch her high chair across the kitchen floor when she was bored sitting in one spot.

Amber didn't like the name her brother gave her. These days, she didn't like her brother much at all. He was always teasing her.

Anyway, Amber didn't need a nickname. She loved her name—Amber Gillian Cantrell. Everyone always commented on how pretty and unusual it was. Ms. Lovejoy said she had never had an Amber in her class before.

Amber opened her eyes. "I wish we could have Ms. Lovejoy again this year."

"We can't have the same teacher three years in a row," Mindy said. "We were lucky to have her twice."

"Maybe she will teach second and third grades and we can be in her class again," Amber said hopefully. "Anything is possible."

Ms. Lovejoy had been their first-grade teacher. Then they had her again in second grade when Ms. Lovejoy taught a split class, half first-graders and half second-graders. Amber wouldn't have minded being taught by Ms. Lovejoy right on through high school.

Ms. Lovejoy never raised her voice, and she didn't use a "time-out" chair when students misbehaved.

As Amber waited for her father, she tugged at the ends of her hair, trying to make it longer, like her Growing-Hair Barbie. Her greatest wish was to have hair long enough to sit on, but hers wasn't that long yet.

Mindy stood up to stretch her legs. "I don't think your dad is coming."

"Yes, he is!" Amber insisted. "It takes him a long time to get here. He lives way over in Maryland."

"Maybe he forgot."

"No, he didn't. He promised to take us to the carnival. He'll be here. You don't know him like I do." But she felt a twinge in the pit of her stomach.

Mindy's family had moved into the house across from Amber's two years ago, the week before the girls started first grade. Amber had hidden beneath the branches of the willow tree in her front yard, watching the movers haul boxes and furniture. She'd been interested in the red-haired girl who looked about her age. Carriage Street had been busy that week. The Alexander family moved in—and Amber's father moved out.

Amber didn't understand why her father didn't want to live with them in Virginia anymore. He'd moved to an apartment in Maryland when he and Amber's mother got a divorce. At first, Amber and

Justin saw their father on weekends and vacations. Then Mr. Cantrell got a new job that meant he had to make a lot of trips to Philadelphia. Now he often cancelled his weekend visits. Amber had hardly seen him all summer. Her stomach hurt whenever she thought about her father.

Mr. Cantrell had called Friday evening, offering to take Amber and Mindy to the Labor Day carnival, to make up for missed weekends. Amber talked about the carnival all weekend, eager to see her father again.

The willow tree's shadow was over the stoop now. It was late. Where was he?

"The next car will be his," Amber predicted, the twinge in her stomach biting deeper. "The veerrry neexxt car..." But the next car wasn't his.

"Amber." Mrs. Cantrell came to the door. "Your father called."

Amber leaped up. "Is he on his way?"

"He just got back from Philadelphia. The holiday traffic on I-270 is terrible. If he left this minute, it would still take him over an hour to get here. I told him it was too late—"

"But he *promised*!" Amber wailed, not caring if Mindy heard.

"—because tomorrow is the first day of school. So Mindy's father will take you girls to the carnival. He'll be right over." Mrs. Cantrell gave Amber a quick hug.

"Your dad said he was really sorry. I'm sorry, too, honey."

Amber sniffed back her tears. She wanted to go to the carnival and she was going. But she wanted to go with her father. He'd *promised*.

Across the street, Mindy's father signaled for them to get into the mini-van. Mindy's little sister Karen was already in the front seat. Mrs. Alexander was staying home with the baby.

"Now where's Justin?" Mrs. Cantrell raised her voice, seeing him shooting baskets in a neighbor's yard. "Justin! Are you going to the carnival?"

Justin ran over, his dark hair spiked with sweat. "Where's Dad? I don't see his car."

"He's not coming," Amber reported glumly. "Mindy's dad is taking us."

"Hurry!" Mindy cried, running across the street.

Amber wasn't in such a rush anymore. She picked up her stuffed raccoon, which was propped against the steps. It was wearing a straw hat with holes cut in the brim for its ears and a dress that had once belonged to Amber's Cabbage Patch doll.

"I'm taking R.C.," she told her mother. Sometimes her stuffed raccoon was the only thing that made that twinge in her stomach go away.

"Oh, honey, don't you think you'd better leave R.C. at home? You might lose her on one of the rides."

"I won't lose her." Amber gripped the raccoon

11

firmly around its furry middle. She dashed across Carriage Street and climbed into the van's back seat beside Mindy.

"Oh, you brought R.C.," Mindy commented. "I should have brought Pearl." Pearl was Mindy's stuffed penguin.

"Dopey girls, carrying stuffed animals everywhere," Justin said.

"R.C. isn't just a stuffed animal," Amber said frostily.

Amber's father had given her the raccoon on her sixth birthday, the summer he'd moved out of the house on Carriage Street. After her father left, the raccoon became Amber's favorite toy. Even though her father had given her lots of presents since the divorce, Amber loved R.C. best.

The carnival was held at the fire station in Fairfax City. Karen squealed when she saw the lights of the Ferris wheel turning lazily against the dusky September sky. Mr. Alexander parked the van on the grass. At the gate, he gave them each a strip of tickets for games and rides. Justin ran off with some friends from school. Mr. Alexander took Karen to ride on the merry-go-round. Amber and Mindy clambered aboard the merry-go-round too, even though there were more exciting rides everywhere they looked.

Amber propped R.C. on the saddle in front of her, enjoying the superior feeling of riding without having to hold on to the pole. Around her, little kids clutched their poles tightly. It felt good to be eight and going into the third grade.

The merry-go-round began to slow down. Amber and Mindy slid off their horses before the ride came to a complete stop. As they leaped off the platform, Amber saw David Jackson and Henry Hoffstedder sharing a huge cloud of cotton candy.

Mindy saw them too. "It's David and Henry."

"Quick!" Amber squealed. "Don't let them see us!"

But the boys were already sauntering in their direction.

"Riding the baby rides?" Henry jeered. Amber didn't like Henry. When he started to poke R.C. with a sticky finger, she jerked her raccoon out of reach.

"Isn't that the raccoon you brought to school last year?" David asked.

Amber nodded. David was okay when he wasn't hanging around that awful Henry Hoffstedder.

"Do you still make neat things like you showed us last year?" David wanted to know. "Those little books and things for your raccoon?"

"Baby stuff," Henry scoffed.

"I can't tell you," Amber said.

"Why not?" asked David.

"Because...it's a secret," she said.

"Who cares?" Henry thrust the syrupy cotton candy cone at David. "Let's go." They ran over to the

Octopus ride.

"Why did you tell them it was a secret?" Mindy asked.

"Because what we did this summer isn't any of their business."

The first day of summer vacation, Amber had walked over to Mindy's house with R.C. and her bag of supplies—crayons, paper, stickers, and markers. Mindy had been sitting on the patio with an assortment of toys around her.

"Are you going to play with R.C. today?" Mindy had asked.

"R.C. wants a catalog to read by the pool. Our catalogs are too big. So I'm making her a raccoon catalog."

Mindy had watched, fascinated, as Amber pasted stickers into a two-inch stapled booklet. "Can I make one too?"

Amber had looked at her. "R.C. really needs a best friend. Do you have a stuffed raccoon that could be her friend?"

"I have a penguin. Her name is Pearl."

So the girls had spent the summer making things for their stuffed animals—miniature toys, clothes, and books. They didn't play with their other toys, only the stuffed raccoon and penguin. It had been a magical time for Amber, wrapped up in a private world with her best friend. She hated to see it end.

They wandered over to a booth where a man was making name tags and buttons. Suddenly Amber had an idea, a way to preserve the magic of summer.

"Let's have buttons made with our secret club on them," Amber said. "We can wear them to school tomorrow!"

"We don't have a secret club," Mindy pointed out.

"Yes, we do. R.C. and Pearl. All that stuff we made for them...it's like a secret club, when you think about it."

"We have to have a name," Mindy said.

"How about their initials? R.C. and P. Nobody will ever guess what it stands for!"

The man made them each a big red button with the initials "R.C. and P." written in bold black letters. They pinned the buttons to their shirts.

Suddenly Amber couldn't wait for the first day of school. Not only would she have the prettiest name and the longest hair, she'd also have a terrific secret the other kids would all want to know about.

Chapter
TWO

The next morning Amber got up before her mother called her and put on the new outfit she had chosen herself when they had gone school shopping the week before. Ignoring the neon-colored short skirts and flouncy dresses, Amber had picked out pink-and-green flowered overalls and a pink T-shirt.

She pinned the red "R.C. and P." button to one overall strap where it could easily be seen. Then she made her bed, pulling her quilt up over the tangled sheets. She thought making her bed every day was a waste of time. She'd just mess it up again that night. Amber placed R.C. against her pillow.

"See you later," she whispered. If her brother walked by her door and heard her talking to a stuffed animal, he'd tease her no end.

R.C. smiled at her. The raccoon never changed expression. It was always in a good mood.

"Breakfast!" her mother yelled from the kitchen.

Amber grabbed her notebook off her dresser, stuffed it in her backpack, then cast a farewell glance at her raccoon. She remembered that wonderful day last year, at the end-of-school assembly. Her one day of fame.

Ms. Lovejoy's class had put on a pageant about the environment. Amber was a tree in the Big Forest. She'd brought R.C. to school so she would have something to hang on to in front of all those people. Ms. Lovejoy thought the raccoon was so cute, she let Amber stand in the first row on the stage.

"You were the star!" her father had said to her afterward. He had come all the way from Maryland in the middle of the week, just to see Amber in the pageant.

Amber had never been happier, especially when the girls in her class gathered around to pet R.C. She showed them the miniature book she had made, a raccoon-sized storybook. The girls were enchanted and even the boys were interested.

From that moment until the end of school, Amber was the most popular kid in her class. Every day she brought something she'd made for R.C. and showed the others.

That was what David had meant last night at the carnival when he asked if she was still making things. Wouldn't he be surprised to learn she and Mindy had created a whole world around their stuffed animals this summer? But he wouldn't find out—not for a while. She would keep it a secret, a tantalizing secret the other kids would be dying to find out about. This year, she would be just as popular.

"Amber!" her mother called again, her voice raspy with exasperation.

Amber ran out to the kitchen. "I'm buying lunch, don't forget," she said to Mrs. Cantrell, who was bagging sandwiches.

"This isn't your lunch. It's your brother's. Justin, you'll need a suitcase to carry all this."

At the table, Justin shoveled cereal into his mouth. "I'm bulking up. I want to go out for wrestling this year."

Amber sat down to a bowl of Cheerios. Justin stared at the button pinned to her strap.

" 'R.C. and P.' What does that mean?"

"None of your beeswax," Amber replied smugly. The button was working already.

"I bet it has something to do with that dorky raccoon."

"Mom, make Justin quit saying stuff about my raccoon."

"Justin, quit saying stuff about Amber's raccoon,"

Mrs. Cantrell recited dutifully.

Justin grabbed his lunch. "See you guys." He dashed out the door to catch the bus to the junior high.

Her mother sat down in Justin's chair. "If you're finished, let me fix your hair."

Mrs. Cantrell brushed Amber's long brown hair until the ends crackled with electricity. Deftly she pulled back a lock from over each ear and fastened a pink-flowered elastic around the ponytail, making a perky plume. Amber bobbed her head like a circus pony.

"Your hair is getting so long," Mrs. Cantrell remarked. "Don't you want to cut it short like Mindy's?"

"No way!"

Her mother laughed. "I know you love long hair. But it *is* a lot of trouble."

"Not to me." Amber tossed her head to make her hair swing out. "Nobody has hair as long as mine."

"Nobody screeches like you do on hair-washing day, either," her mother said wryly. "Better scoot. The bus'll be here any minute. Remember, you go to Mindy's after school."

"Mondays, Tuesdays, Thursdays, and Fridays," Amber chanted. Those were the days her mother kept her quilt shop open until six. On Wednesdays, the shop closed early and her mother was there when

Amber got home from school.

Mrs. Cantrell walked Amber to the door. "Your dad said he'd be here early on Saturday and for you to think about what you'd like to do. He was really sorry about missing the carnival last night."

Amber felt that twinge in her stomach again. Every time her father was late or didn't show up, her stomach gave a pull, like yanking down a window shade. Now she felt the twinge whenever her father was mentioned.

"I just remembered!" Amber cried, running back to her room. She dashed back out with R.C. "Me and Mindy are having play school after real school today. Bye, Mom!"

"Mindy and *I*," her mother said, giving her a kiss.

Amber flew across Carriage Street, her hair streaming out behind her. Mindy was pacing on her front porch.

"I hear the bus on Buggy Whip!" she shouted, opening the door. Amber raced inside Mindy's house and tossed R.C. on the sofa next to Mindy's penguin, then raced out the door again. Their bus was just pulling up to the curb.

"Made it with time to spare," Amber said as the girls piled into an empty seat. "I thought we'd make little notebooks out of lined paper." When Mindy gave her a blank look, she added, "For our play school. And we can make little spelling books and math dittos. So our animals can do what we're doing this year."

Mindy slid her pink backpack, identical to the one Amber carried, off her shoulder. "Do you think we'll have time for all that? I bet we have a ton of homework. Third grade is a lot harder than second grade."

"It can't be *that* much harder. Did anybody say anything about your button?"

Mindy tilted the red button pinned to her T-shirt so she could read the slogan. "My mom asked what it meant."

"You didn't tell her, did you?"

"Yeah. Why not?"

"Mindy! It's supposed to be a secret!" At Mindy's stricken look, Amber said, "Okay, we can tell our parents, but nobody else. When kids ask you what 'R.C. and P.' means, say it's a secret and we aren't allowed to tell. It'll be fun."

A dozen buses formed a golden river in front of Virginia Run Elementary. Amber and Mindy hopped off their bus and ran up the steps into the main building. "Welcome, Virginia Run Students!" proclaimed a banner stretched across the archway leading to the office.

"I love school," Amber said, happily hugging her backpack. "I love every little thing about it."

She didn't really love *every* little thing about

school—she loved the newness of the first day. The building was clean and welcoming; the teachers and staff were smiling. Even the kids looked new in their crisp back-to-school outfits and unmarked sneakers.

"Let's go find our room," Mindy said.

A few days earlier, the students had received letters with their room assignments. Amber and Mindy had compared letters and learned they were in the same class again.

Mindy pointed. "There it is. Room Six."

"Wait a sec." Amber paused at the door of another classroom. "Let's say hi to Ms. Lovejoy."

The teacher was kneeling by her desk, wiping the tears of a little girl. Ms. Lovejoy glanced up and saw her former students standing in the doorway.

"Amber! And Mindy! Look, class, two of my old students have come to visit."

A thrill rippled up Amber's spine as the little kids regarded her with open admiration and awe. To them, she was an *old student*, someone who knew her way around this place. Being a third-grader was going to be wonderful!

"We just wanted to say hi," Amber said. "Hi."

"Hi," Mindy echoed.

Ms. Lovejoy came over. She wore a flowered dress that made her look like a moving garden. "Did you have a nice summer? You're both so tall! Amber, turn around." Amber twirled, making the ends of her hair fly out. "Your hair is so long!"

"I've been growing it all summer," Amber said proudly.

"I bet you have the longest hair of any girl in this school. What room are you in?"

"Six," Amber and Mindy both answered.

Ms. Lovejoy nodded. "Mrs. Sharp's class. She's great."

"I bet she won't be as nice as you," Amber said loyally.

Ms. Lovejoy laughed and gave them each a quick squeeze. "It was wonderful seeing you. Stop by and visit anytime."

The bell was about to ring, so they hurried to Room Six.

"Hey," Mindy exclaimed. "There's that dumb old Henry Hoffstedder."

"And David Jackson," Amber added. "I hope *he's* not in our class. But I think he is."

Secretly, Amber pretended David Jackson was her boyfriend. Last year, he'd sat behind her and pulled her hair. Once he tied the ends together. It took Amber's mother two hours to untangle the mess. David probably liked her. Why else would he pull her hair?

Now she dramatically bunched her long hair in one hand as she and Mindy swept by David and Henry Hoffstedder. The boys made rude sounds as the girls passed. David swiped at Amber's hair.

"Get away!" she squealed, her heart pounding with excitement. David still liked her!

An older woman in a navy blue skirt and white blouse sat at the desk. The new teacher didn't look a bit like Ms. Lovejoy. Her short hair was gray and black mixed together and she wore glasses. Her name was printed in neat block letters on the blackboard: Elvira Sharp.

Amber felt sorry for her new teacher. How awful to be saddled with a clunky name and short, gray-and-black hair. Mrs. Sharp would probably appreciate having Amber in the room.

"Let's sit over there," Amber said to Mindy, choosing desks next to each other. Amber felt it was her duty to sit near the front. The teacher could look over at Amber anytime and be cheered by the sight of the girl with the long brown hair and pretty name.

The late bell rang. The teacher rose from her seat to close the door. "My name is Mrs. Sharp," she began. She had a no-nonsense voice and darting eyes that wouldn't miss a thing.

Some of Amber's excitement ebbed away. Mrs. Sharp was going to be strict.

"I'll call the roll now. Raise your hand when I say your name. That way I will learn who you are. Mindy Alexander."

"Here." Mindy raised her hand.

"Bryan Bean."

A few students giggled. Amber giggled too. Bryan Bean was a funny name. She was glad *she* didn't have a funny name.

"Carly Brown."

A thin girl with blond hair raised her hand and said, "Here."

Amber remembered Carly from Ms. Lovejoy's class last year. A lot of the kids looked familiar. There were some new faces, too.

Amber got ready to raise her hand when the teacher reached her name. Though Mrs. Sharp hadn't said much so far, Amber knew she would remark what a pretty name Amber had and smile specially at her.

But when Mrs. Sharp called out "Amber Cantrell," she merely nodded at Amber and said matter-of-factly, "I have an Amber in my class almost every year."

Amber pulled her arm down as if she'd been stung. How could there be more than one Amber? She pictured a row of Amber Cantrells, like robots, sitting in other classrooms.

"Henry Hoffstedder." Mrs. Sharp went on with the roll. "David Jackson."

Amber looked around to see where David was sitting. He hadn't chosen the seat behind Amber this year. Lisa Lee had taken that desk. David was clear across the room. Why was he way over there?

Then Amber saw the reason. She drew in a breath and didn't let it out.

A girl sat in front of David. Amber had never seen her before. She wore a purple stone-washed skirt and a purple top. But it was the girl's hair that caused Amber to stop breathing.

The girl's hair was the color of honey. It flowed down her back, past her waist, past her hips, like a silky waterfall. The ends of her hair curled around the rim of her chair seat. Her hair was *long enough to sit on!*

"Who is that girl?" Amber whispered to Mindy. "The one in front of David."

Mindy craned her neck. "I don't know," she whispered back. "I never saw her before."

"Me neither." Amber wished she had never seen the girl at all. She couldn't believe someone with hair longer than hers was actually in the same class! Amber had been so sure she'd have the longest hair in third grade. Maybe the girl had a terrible name. Something even worse than Elvira. Even though Amber didn't have the longest hair, she would still have the prettiest name.

She listened intently to the rest of the roll call, anxious to hear the girl's name. If it wasn't awful, it would probably be something ordinary.

But the girl didn't raise her hand when any of the

ordinary names were called. Mrs. Sharp was into the W's, almost at the end of the roll. She came to a name that made her smile. "Delight Wakefield."

Amber wasn't surprised when the girl with the mile-long hair raised her hand.

"What a beautiful name," the teacher trilled. "I've never had a Delight in my class before."

The other kids looked at Delight with interest. Amber could tell they were eager to get to know the new girl.

Nobody looked at Amber with interest. Amber sagged at her desk. She hadn't been in third grade ten minutes and already she wished she were back in second grade, back in Ms. Lovejoy's class when she had had the prettiest name and the longest hair.

THREE

At lunch, Delight told the class her life story. Spellbound, everyone crowded around Delight's end of the table.

"My parents wanted a baby for years and years," the new girl explained. "And when they finally got me, they were so delighted, that's what they named me."

Amber and Mindy ate by themselves at the other end of the table. Amber tried not to listen, but found herself leaning forward to catch Delight's soft voice.

Amber said crossly to Mindy, "Some people think they are the *only* one with a neat name." She took a bite of pizza, stretching out the cheese until it spun thin as a thread and broke. They always had pizza the first day of school. Usually it tasted good, but today she wasn't very hungry.

Mindy didn't try to hide the fact she was interested in the new girl. "I wonder if she's ever cut her hair. I'm going to ask her."

"Don't!" Amber blurted.

"Why not?"

"Because…" Amber floundered for an excuse. She couldn't stand Delight getting all this attention. If Mindy asked Delight about her hair, she'd probably tell them that she only started growing it last week or something.

"Why can't I ask her?" Mindy pressed.

"Because…because it's a wig!" Amber decided that nobody could have hair as long as Delight's. She'd been growing her own hair forever and it still wasn't long enough to sit on. Delight's hair couldn't be real.

"A wig?" Mindy repeated. "How can you tell?"

"It looks fake, just like Gammy Cantrell's hair."

Amber's great-grandmother wore a wig to cover her sparse white hair. Gammy never put her wig on straight, but slapped it crookedly on her head like a baseball cap. Amber always giggled whenever she saw her great-grandmother's lopsided hair.

Mindy narrowed her eyes at Delight. "I think her hair is real. It looks real to me."

"It isn't," Amber insisted. "See the part? That's the seam."

Underneath the beautiful long wig, Delight

Wakefield probably had short hair. Or maybe no hair. That was it—she was bald!

The others were unaware of Delight's fake hair. They peppered Delight with questions.

"Where did you live before you came to Virginia?" Carly asked.

"Japan," Delight replied.

"Japan! How neat! Can you speak Japanese?"

Delight laughed. "Only a little. I can speak French better. We lived in Paris for three years."

"Where else have you lived?" David wanted to know. David, Bryan, and Henry were clustered around the new girl. Amber couldn't believe it. Usually the boys sat as far away from the girls as they could.

On her fingers, Delight ticked off the places she had lived. "Japan, France. Turkey, for a few months. Germany before that. I was born in Germany."

"I bet the schools were hard," said Lisa.

Delight shook her head. "I went to American schools. They spoke English. But I had French lessons at the school in Paris."

"We're going to learn French," Amber put in. "From TV. Mrs. Sharp said so."

Before lunch, Mrs. Sharp had told the class some of the things they would be doing that year. They would learn French from educational TV. They would study science and math and reading and social studies. Mrs. Sharp passed out textbooks. Most of their books had been used before, but the social studies textbook was brand-new. It was called *Other Roads, Other Neighborhoods*. Amber had leafed through it blindly, still reeling from the shock of a girl in her class with longer hair and a prettier name.

Now Delight smiled in Amber's direction. "That'll be fun. We can talk to each other in French." Then she spied the big red button pinned to Amber's overall strap. "What does your button say?"

Amber glanced down as if she'd forgotten all about the button. "Oh, this. It says 'R.C. and P.' Mindy and me had these made special."

The other kids twisted in their seats. For the first time that day, their attention was fastened on Amber and Mindy.

"What does it stand for?" asked Carly.

Amber smiled. The kids would forget about Delight when they heard about the secret club. After a dramatic pause, she replied, "I can't tell you. It's the name of our secret club."

"Secret club!" Lisa echoed.

Now Amber was pelted with questions.

"What's it about?"

"Who's in it?"

"Well," Amber dragged out the word to whet their appetites. "Only two people so far. Me and Mindy."

Henry Hoffstedder frowned at Amber's button.

"'R.C. and P.' I bet I know what those initials stand for."

"What?" Amber challenged. Henry didn't know that she and Mindy had created a special world for their toys that summer. He'd never guess in a million years.

"I bet R.C. has something to do with that stupid raccoon you drag everywhere..."

David slapped the table with his hand. "R.C. is its name! You're right. It's a club about stuffed animals!" The boys hooted.

"It's a *fantastic* club, isn't it, Mindy?" Amber prompted. "We do all sorts of neat stuff. *Secret* stuff."

"I bet," Henry mocked. "It can't be much of a club with only two people in it."

Amber realized she shouldn't have made the club sound so exclusive. Hastily she added, "We were going to let other kids join. But only *certain* kids can be in it. No boys."

"We wouldn't be in your dopey club if you paid us a hundred dollars," Henry threw back.

Delight spoke up. "I think a club is a neat idea. Why don't we start a class club? A lunch table club. We could hold meetings at lunch every day."

"Yeah," David seconded. "And we'll leave *those* two out." He pointed at Amber and Mindy. Amber wondered why she had ever thought David Jackson would make a good boyfriend. He wasn't nice at all!

"It's a class club," Delight said firmly. "Anybody can join."

Everyone began talking at once about Delight's new Lunch Table Club. No one was interested in Amber's club anymore.

"I'm afraid we can't join," Amber declared. When the others were looking at her again, she said, "Our club keeps us very busy. We won't have time for two clubs, will we, Mindy?" She kicked Mindy under the table.

"No," Mindy agreed with a dark look at Amber.

"Are you sure?" Delight asked. "You have to eat lunch."

"We're sure." Amber ignored Mindy's look.

"Good." David wadded his lunch bag. "We didn't want you in our club anyway."

"I think Delight should be president," Carly said, pushing her chair closer to Delight's. It was obvious Carly was angling to be Delight's best friend.

"Yeah," chimed Lisa. "Delight is president!"

Amber finished her lunch in misery. This wasn't how it was supposed to go at all! The kids were supposed to beg to join *her* club. Instead, they were clamoring to get in Delight's club.

The kids were intrigued by Delight because she was new, Amber figured. And she had lived all over the world. Or so she claimed. Amber didn't quite believe her. Anything was possible, but some of the things Delight said seemed far-fetched. She could be making it all up just to get attention. She was probably a fake, Amber concluded, like her hair.

Maybe if the other kids found out Delight was a fake, they'd forget about her dumb Lunch Table Club. They'd want to be in Amber's club instead.

Just then, Delight pushed her long, honey-colored hair over her shoulder. If only someone would pull Delight's hair, they'd see it was a wig. One yank, and Delight would be revealed as a phony.

But who would do that? Amber was the only one who suspected Delight was wearing a wig. She bit her bottom lip. She would have to pull off Delight's wig. It was the only way.

Before she lost her nerve, Amber leaped up from her chair and ran over to Delight's end of the table.

"Hold still, you have a spider in your hair," she cried.

Delight shrieked and clutched her head. "I do? Where?"

"Move your hands, I'll get it." Amber tugged gingerly at a hank of Delight's hair. It was probably glued on. She tugged harder. The other girl's hair didn't budge. Was the wig cemented to her head?

"Ow!" Delight wailed. "Did you get it?"

"Yeah, I got it." Amber stared woefully at the part in Delight's hair. It wasn't a seam.

Delight Wakefield's long, beautiful hair was definitely real.

"I've made two notebooks each," Mindy said, holding out miniature pads of paper, stapled at the top. "Is that enough?"

They were working in Mindy's living room. Sarah, the baby, was lying on her back in the porta-crib, trying to chew her toes. Karen was watching cartoons on TV.

Amber looked up from her magazine. "I guess so. Now you can start on the cursive workbooks."

Mindy tossed her scissors to the floor. "I'm tired of making books."

"I've got the worst job," Amber countered. "Try doing the social studies book and see how easy that is."

Her own social studies textbook, *Other Roads, Other Neighborhoods,* was open on the coffee table. It was filled with pictures of people working and playing.

Amber flipped through a bunch of Mrs. Alexander's magazines, hunting for tiny pictures of raccoons and penguins working and playing. So far she had found only one penguin picture.

"Can't we do something else?" Mindy asked crossly.

"I thought you wanted to play school with R.C.

and Pearl. You said so this morning."

"I want to play school, but all we ever do is *make* things and it takes forever. Why can't we just play without making stuff first?"

To Amber, making things was the best part. She liked the special closeness she and Mindy had shared when they had made things for their stuffed animals this summer. They'd only been in school one day and that summer closeness seemed to be disappearing. But making a tiny social studies textbook wasn't much fun, she had to admit.

She closed her magazine. "What do you want to do?"

"Let's go out. I'm sick of being indoors."

"Okay. We'll take R.C. and Pearl for a ride. I'll go get my bike." They could play school another day, Amber decided.

She ran across the street and wheeled her bike from the garage, then put R.C. in the white wicker basket and coasted down her driveway. Mindy was already there, with her penguin perched in her bike basket.

"Where are we going?" she asked Amber. "I have to be back soon to watch Sarah while Mom fixes dinner."

"Let's ride over the bridge."

They pedaled down Carriage Street. The September sunshine was warm, but not too hot.

Amber liked the way their stuffed animals rode perkily in their bike baskets and caused people to look at them. Mothers pushing strollers smiled as they passed.

Carriage Street was the longest street in their section of town. It crossed over Little Rocky Run, the stream that separated the houses of Creekside, where Amber and Mindy lived, from the newer, bigger houses of Mockingbird Ridge.

When Amber and Mindy reached the bridge, they parked their bikes next to the concrete pilings. They liked to lean over the rail and gaze at the brown water swirling below. Once they'd seen a pair of beavers swimming downstream, their sleek brown heads bobbing in the water. Farther downstream, the beavers had built a dam of branches. Sometimes Amber and Mindy threw sticks into the creek, so the beavers would have a ready supply whenever they needed to repair their dam.

Today the girls just hung over the rail, enjoying the warmth of the sun. A shiny silver bicycle crested the hill of Mockingbird Ridge. A girl with a mile-long ponytail whizzed toward them. It was Delight Wakefield.

"Hi!" she said, hopping off her bike. "Do you guys live here, too?"

"We live down there," Mindy answered, pointing. "On the other side of the creek."

"We're practically in the same neighborhood." Delight spotted Amber's raccoon in her bike basket. "Oh, how cute! Can I pick him up?"

"It's a she," Amber corrected. "And she's taking a nap. Don't bother her."

Delight laughed. "A stuffed animal taking a nap! That's funny. I have a stuffed animal, too. It's a dog my mom bought me in Paris. I named him Row-bear. That's French for Robert."

"A dog from France," Mindy said, awestruck. "Could we see him sometime?"

"My raccoon came from someplace foreign, too," Amber put in.

"Maryland," Mindy said with a snort. "Big deal."

"Yeah, but it came from a foreign country *before* it got to Maryland. I don't remember which one. My dad bought it for me and he told me, but I forget," Amber said to Delight.

"Maybe we can get together with our stuffed animals," Delight suggested, flinging back that wonderful hair. "They could have a party or something."

Mindy brightened. "That sounds like fun!"

"R.C. is busy," Amber said coolly. "Every single day of the week. You should see her calendar. It's full."

For a second Delight looked disappointed. Then she laughed again. "A stuffed raccoon with an appointment calendar! You're too much, Amber. Well, I have to get home. See you guys tomorrow."

She jumped back on her bicycle and pedaled up the hill, turning once to wave.

"She's nice, isn't she?" Mindy said. "Not stuck up or anything."

Amber didn't agree. Had Mindy fallen under Delight's spell, too, like everyone else in their class?

How do you like third grade?" Mr. Cantrell asked Amber.

"It's okay." Amber toyed with her hamburger, looking around to see if Justin was coming back to their table.

It had not been a good day. Mr. Cantrell had arrived late at Amber's house, and they missed the first showing of the movie Amber had chosen. Then Justin decided he didn't want to watch Amber's picture and declared he was going to see the R-rated movie next door instead. Mr. Cantrell told Justin they were going to watch a movie together, as a family, and Justin retorted they weren't a family anymore, so what was the point? Justin reluctantly followed them into Amber's movie when it finally started, but refused to sit with them. After the movie, they walked over to Fantastic Friday for hamburgers. Justin immediately stationed himself by the video games, leaving Amber alone with their father.

"Just okay?" Mr. Cantrell persisted. "I thought you were really looking forward to school this year."

Amber slowly chewed a French fry. She knew her father was mad at Justin. The whole day was spoiled. "It's not as fun as I thought it would be," she said.

"I remember third grade," Mr. Cantrell said, surprising Amber. Could her father remember back that far? "My teacher was Mrs. Stann. I liked her a lot. And there was this kid...what was her name? Julie! She was a ball of fire. Mrs. Stann picked her to be the star of our class play. She was so popular. I was nuts about her."

Her father smiled, fondly recalling Julie, the third-grade ball of fire. A loud electronic *boing! boing! boing!* and Justin's "All right!" made him turn around. He frowned.

"Seven bucks down the drain," he muttered, referring to Justin's uneaten dinner.

Amber hastily finished her own hamburger. She wanted to tell her father exactly why she wasn't thrilled about third grade, but it was time to go. He wasn't in a listening mood anyway.

In the car all the way home, her father and brother argued. Amber sat quietly in the front seat, wondering how she'd ever get her father's attention.

When she kissed him good-bye at the curb in front of their house, her father held her close and said, "Sorry about today, Pumpkin. Next week will be better, okay?"

Amber breathed in the outdoorsy smell of his jacket. "Okay," she said.

But the next weekend her father had to go to Philadelphia.

"Today is Trade Day," Amber declared on the bus one morning.

"I think we're going out to eat tonight," Mindy said.

"Then I get to go in your place," Amber said cheerfully. "We have to trade everything. That's the rule."

"You also get to walk Sarah if she starts fussing," Mindy added. "Plus you have to take my math makeup test."

The tradition of Trade Day began last summer. One hot afternoon, the girls were so bored they decided to trade lives for a whole day. They swapped clothes, barrettes, and shoes. They exchanged books and toys. At suppertime, they went to each other's houses and sat in each other's places at the table.

On the first Trade Day, Mrs. Cantrell was startled to see Mindy sitting in Amber's chair, but Mrs.

Alexander called and said she was all for the temporary switch. Amber kept Mindy's little sisters entertained. She enjoyed being the oldest in the family. And it was nice having a father at the dinner table again.

Trade Day worked fine in the summer, but maybe they would have to make some changes now that school had started.

"Okay," Amber relented, not wanting to do Mindy's makeup test. "Part Trade Day."

As the bus jostled along, they modified the rules. They would switch everything but homework and names. They knew Mrs. Sharp would not stand for that kind of foolishness. After school, they would swap games and snacks, but Trade Day would officially end at suppertime.

At school, they passed their classmates playing on the blacktop and went straight to the girls' room to change outfits before the bell. When they emerged, giggling because Amber's shoes were too small for Mindy, Delight was lingering by the water fountain. She stared at them.

"Didn't I see *you* wearing those pants a minute ago?" she asked Amber. "And weren't *you* wearing her skirt?" she said to Mindy.

"Mmmmmm...could be, Doc." Amber's imitation of Bugs Bunny set the girls off again.

Delight laughed. "I get it! You traded clothes!"

"It's Trade Day," Mindy explained. "We did this last summer and it was really fun. We trade our clothes, lunches, everything."

Delight's blue eyes were shining. "I wish I could trade with you sometime."

"It wouldn't work with three," Amber said. "Only two. Come on, Mindy. We have to switch desks."

They left Delight standing there. "I bet Mrs. Sharp won't let you!" she sang after them.

"Why did you tell her it wouldn't work with three?" Mindy demanded. "It would too work. I could trade with you and you could trade with Delight, and Delight could trade with me."

"That's too complicated," Amber said. She wasn't about to trade anything with Delight Wakefield.

Delight was right about one thing, though. Mrs. Sharp would not let them switch desks.

"Your seat was assigned to you at the beginning of the year. It's your space, like your house in your neighborhood."

They had to be content swapping notebooks, pencils, and textbooks. At lunchtime, they traded lunches.

"I got the better deal today," Amber crowed, pulling a slice of cake from Mindy's lunch box.

Mindy wasn't listening. She munched Amber's tuna sandwich while gazing enviously at Delight's Lunch Table Club at the other end of the long table.

Everyone had pooled their lunches in the center of the table and was snatching bits and pieces of sandwiches and chips, like a picnic. Their laughter brought warning glances from the monitor.

"That looks like fun," Mindy said wistfully.

Amber made a scornful sound. "They just copied us."

"Maybe. But it looks like more fun with a lot of people. I wouldn't mind joining Delight's club."

"We have our *own* club and it's a lot better than theirs. We have something they don't have—R.C. and Pearl," Amber reminded her.

But it was hard keeping a club going with only two members. Amber still hoped other kids would get bored with Delight's club and join hers. If only they could see the neat world she and Mindy had created for their stuffed animals!

But Amber knew some of the other kids would make fun of them for playing with stuffed animals. The special magic she and Mindy shared all summer would be ruined. More than anything—even more than having hair long enough to sit on—Amber didn't want to lose that magic.

"Will these colors make a pretty quilt?" Amber asked. She had spread a number of pink and green fabric scraps on the floor of her mother's sewing room.

Her mother peered over her half-glasses. She was

repairing a Flying Geese quilt she had bought from an old lady in the Blue Ridge Mountains. "Very nice. Be sure all the squares are exactly the same size."

Her mother had promised to make R.C. a miniature patchwork quilt if Amber would cut out the squares.

"Mom, can I talk to you about something?" She'd been waiting all evening to speak to her mother.

"What is it?" her mother said.

"There's this new girl at school," Amber began. "I don't like her very much, but everybody else does." Including Mindy, she thought with a lump in her throat.

"Why don't you like her?" her mother asked.

Amber rocked back on her heels. Where should she start? With Delight's long, longer-than-Amber's hair? Or Delight's wonderful name, prettier than Amber's? Or the fact that Delight had lived all over the world and spoke French?

"She brags," Amber said.

"About what?"

"About living in Paris and having this French dog. And how her parents were so lucky to have her, they named her Delight."

"Delight!" her mother exclaimed. "What a lovely name."

Amber's heart sank. Even her *mother* liked Delight's name. "Is Delight a prettier name than mine?"

"They are both pretty names. Of course, I am partial to Amber." Her mother's voice held a smile.

"Delight started this club," Amber went on. "And she let everybody in the whole class join."

"Very democratic. Did you join?"

"No." Amber looked down at her shoes. "Mindy and me have our own club. But Mindy wants to join Delight's club."

"What's wrong with that?" For once, Mrs. Cantrell did not say "Mindy and *I*."

"We started our club first. Just because Delight came pushing in..." Amber broke off, near tears.

Her mother put down her needle. "I think I know what the problem is. You're afraid Mindy is going to like Delight better than you, am I right?" Amber nodded. "Sweetheart, you and Mindy have been friends since first grade."

"Mindy doesn't like my ideas anymore. She says it's too much work, making things for our animals."

"You and Mindy were thick as thieves all summer. But now school has started and you aren't by yourselves anymore. Let Mindy be friends with someone besides you. She won't dump you. She just wants another friend, that's all."

Amber wasn't so sure. Lately, Mindy acted like she wanted to trade more than clothes and toys. Was Mindy ready to trade Amber for a new best friend?

* * * * *

All the girls in their class were gathered around Delight Wakefield's desk when Amber and Mindy walked into Room Six. Stretching to see over heads, Amber saw the reason for Delight's popularity.

Perched on Delight's desk was a rust-colored stuffed dog. A huge red ribbon was tied in a fancy bow around his neck.

The girls argued over who got to hold him.

Delight stood in the middle of the circle. "You can all have a turn. Everybody will have a chance to pet him."

"What's his name?" asked Lisa.

"Row-bear. It's French for Robert. My mother bought him for me when we lived in Paris. He's lived in three countries! First France, then Japan, and now the United States. My father says he's a well-traveled dog."

Amber noticed that Delight was wearing her hair in a French braid. The end of her braid stopped just above her hips and was tied with a red ribbon to match her dog's. Amber had always wanted to wear her hair like that, but her mother didn't know how to make French braids.

"Look at Delight's dog," Mindy cooed. "Isn't he cute?"

"I can't believe she'd bring a stuffed animal to school," Amber said. "In *third grade*!"

Mrs. Sharp came in then and called the class to order. "Put the dog away," she said to Delight, after taking attendance. "It's time for lessons. Open your *Other Roads, Other Neighborhoods* book to page seven. Read the introduction silently—that means to yourself, Henry and David—and then we'll talk about our projects."

Amber got out her social studies book. She wasn't interested in how other people worked and played. Her eyes skimmed the introduction but she didn't understand a word she read. She was busy thinking how everyone in class would ooh and aah if she brought R.C. to school.

"Is everyone finished?" Mrs. Sharp asked the class. A few kids murmured they were still reading. Delight Wakefield, Amber noted, was one of the ones who needed more time.

"Now that you've read the introduction," Mrs. Sharp said a few minutes later, "you know social studies is all about understanding how people live and work together."

Social studies sounded awfully dull. Amber thought about the kids in Ms. Lovejoy's room. They were probably coloring pictures and singing "She'll Be Comin' 'Round the Mountain."

"You will each write a report about life in your neighborhood," the teacher continued. "I want you to observe the people on your street. Ask them questions. Find out where they work. What they do in their jobs. How they have fun."

Amber's hand shot skyward. "What if we live on the same street?" She pointed to Mindy.

"Yeah," David piped up. "Henry and Carly live on my block."

"Those of you who share the same neighborhood should get together," Mrs. Sharp replied. "Each of you can take a different part. Or maybe your grandparents live nearby. Do your report on your grandparents' neighborhood and let your classmate have the neighborhood you live in. Are there any more questions?"

There weren't any. Mrs. Sharp's brisk manner discouraged too many questions.

"All right. Today's Tuesday, library day. Line up at the door, please."

Because Delight sat near the door, she was always first in line. Every Tuesday, Delight Wakefield led the class to the library. Today, Amber decided *she* would be first.

While Delight was busy putting Row-bear under her chair, Amber ran to the door, beating David, who was also trying to be first.

"No fair running!" David complained.

"You're just jealous because you didn't get here first," Amber told him.

"David and Amber," Mrs. Sharp warned. "No

fighting." Amber firmly held her post as first at the door. She was thrilled to see that Delight was at the very end.

Mrs. Sharp regarded the pushing and shoving in the line. "Everyone, turn so you are facing the windows." Feet shuffled as the third-graders obeyed.

Now the line faced the other way. Amber was puzzled. Were they going to walk to the library backwards?

"The last person in line may lead the way to the library," Mrs. Sharp said.

Delight triumphantly led the class out the door. Amber, now at the very end of the line, was outraged. What a dirty trick!

"Nyah, nyah, nyah," David threw over his shoulder.

Ms. Lovejoy would never play such a rotten trick on her class, Amber thought.

She was beginning to think third grade was not so great after all.

Chapter
FIVE

Room Six was a jungle of stuffed animals.

Bears, cats, and rabbits sat on desk tops. Some of the animals were worn and threadbare. Some were missing an eye or had a torn leg sewn with thick, clumsy stitches. Other stuffed animals were glaringly new, sporting crisp neck ribbons. Amber knew those were the ones that sat on bookshelves or beds and were looked at but not loved.

Mindy's face lit up as they walked into the room. "Hey, neat! Everybody brought stuffed animals today."

Amber didn't see what was so neat about it. She shrugged her pack off her shoulder. R.C.'s ears stuck out from the top flap.

Mindy tugged her penguin from her own

backpack. She propped Pearl on her desk. "I'm glad we brought ours today. Isn't it funny how all the girls brought stuffed animals?"

Amber didn't think it was funny at all. Yesterday at Mindy's house she told Mindy they were bringing their animals to school, so the kids could see what *special* stuffed animals looked like. But how could anyone see how special R.C. was in that forest of ordinary toys?

Delight Wakefield strolled up and down the aisles, carrying Row-bear. The girls practically fell over themselves to show their stuffed animals to Delight.

"I only keep him on my bed," Lisa was explaining, as she finger-combed the mane of a stuffed lion. "I don't *play* with him anymore."

"I don't play with Row-bear, either," Delight said. "He's sort of like an old friend."

The boys didn't like being left out. David grabbed Carly's bear and pitched it to Henry, who tossed it to Bryan.

"Give him back!" Carly cried. "I'm telling Mrs. Sharp!"

Bryan was a feeble keep-away player. He threw the bear to Carly, who checked him over for damage. The bear was very old, Amber could see. One ear had been chewed off.

"His name is Growler," Carly told Delight. "My grandmother brought him from England before I was born."

"Oh, he's cute," Delight said. "It's so great seeing all our old toys together. Look, Amber and Mindy brought theirs too. Did I tell you guys to bring in your stuffed animals? I don't remember."

So it *was* Delight's idea to bring stuffed animals to school, Amber thought sourly. And she had everyone do it on the very day that Amber decided to bring in R.C. Nobody was paying any attention to Amber's raccoon.

"How's R.C., Amber?" Delight asked. "Taken her for a bike ride lately?"

"Amber takes that raccoon *everywhere*," David said. The other boys began to tease her.

Amber flushed. She was relieved when Mrs. Sharp turned from the blackboard where she had been writing their morning lesson and said, "Take your seats, please, everyone. Didn't you hear the bell? And put your playthings away, girls. This is a classroom, not a toy store."

The girls stowed their stuffed animals in the cubbies under their desks. But Amber scrunched over in her seat to make room for R.C. Her raccoon was not going to be crammed under any old desk.

Mindy saw the stuffed animal sitting next to her. "You didn't put R.C. away."

"I know. I don't want her to get all dirty under my desk."

"Mrs. Sharp's going to get mad."

"Maybe she won't see her." Amber tucked the stuffed raccoon under her elbow.

"We will begin with social studies," Mrs. Sharp said, after calling roll.

This was no surprise. They started every day with social studies. Mrs. Sharp stuck to a schedule that had not changed since the first week of school.

Ms. Lovejoy never did the same thing two days in a row, Amber remembered. If they had reading first one day, they would have reading in the afternoon the next day. And they *always* began the day with something fun, like coloring or singing. Mrs. Sharp believed in getting down to business right off.

With a sigh, Amber opened her social studies book.

"We're going to work on our neighborhood projects," Mrs. Sharp was saying. "I want you to write a paragraph about your neighborhood. Tell me what it looks like. How many houses are on your street? Who lives in the houses, and what do those people do? You may illustrate with pictures showing the jobs of the people in your neighborhood. There are magazines up here. You are welcome to cut pictures from them."

Amber perked up. Making booklets was one of her favorite activities. She was an expert, after all the magazines and books she had made for her raccoon.

Mrs. Sharp set out construction paper and glue next to the pile of magazines. Then she instructed the first row to come up front. Ms. Lovejoy always let *her* class stampede the activity table. She didn't care if her students made a little noise.

Delight's row was first, naturally. Delight led her group to the front as if she were leading a parade. Amber saw her speak to Mrs. Sharp, who nodded. Then Delight came over to Amber's seat, clutching three glossy magazines.

"I was wondering," Delight began hesitantly. "Since we live in the same neighborhood, maybe we could work together on our reports."

Amber stared at her. Delight, the girl who had ruined Amber's chance to show the class what a special stuffed animal looked like, wanted to work with her on the social studies project?

"We don't live in the same neighborhood," Amber pointed out. "Mindy and me live in Creekside. You live in Mockingbird Ridge."

"But it's just over the creek," Delight said. "It's the same street."

"She's right," Mindy said to Amber. "She lives on Carriage Street same as we do."

"But *way* at the other end." Amber made it sound as if Delight lived on the edge of the earth. "Mindy and me are working on our reports together. You'll have to do yours by yourself."

Delight did not like being turned away. "I should have known better than to ask *you*, Amber Cantrell." She saw the raccoon under Amber's arm. "You didn't put your stuffed animal away."

"It's none of your beeswax," Amber said, trying to hide R.C.

Their voices were raised just enough to alert Mrs. Sharp's disapproving ear. She bustled toward them.

"What's going on here? Delight, please go back to your seat." As Delight returned to her desk, Mrs. Sharp's keen eyes spied Amber's raccoon sitting beside her. "I thought I told you to put your playthings away. Since you can't follow directions, I'll have to hold your toy until the end of the day."

Amber was horrified. Hand over her raccoon to be locked in Mrs. Sharp's dark supply cupboard? It was unthinkable.

"I'll put her under my desk," she said, hoping Mrs. Sharp would change her mind.

"No, you won't. You had a chance to do that earlier, but you chose to do otherwise. The toy is clearly a distraction. I'll put it in my cupboard for safekeeping. You may claim it at the end of the day."

Amber reluctantly surrendered her raccoon. She watched with miserable eyes as her teacher locked R.C. in the supply cabinet.

When Amber's row finally walked up front to get magazines, Amber saw only the crummy ones were left. Tattered magazines that had been used for previous classroom projects lay in an unappealing heap on the table. Amber snatched at a falling-apart *National Geographic.* Delight probably took the best magazines. At least Amber had prevented Delight from working on the project with her and Mindy.

"Here's how we should divide our neighborhood," Amber said to Mindy. "I'll take the side of the street my house is on, and you do your side."

Mindy frowned. "All the good people are on your side of the street. Nobody interesting lives on my side. Mr. Appleton the dentist. And Mr. Potts. He cleans out septic tanks. Big thrill."

Amber couldn't help it if she had a vet and a Secret Service agent living on her side of the street.

"How about splitting the street in half?" Mindy suggested. "Then we each have houses on both sides of the street."

"How?"

"You take the houses from your house to the corner of Horsepen, and I'll take the houses from my house to the corner of Buggy Whip."

Amber almost agreed. Then she remembered the Secret Service agent lived at the corner of Buggy Whip. The vet lived two doors down, on Amber's side of the street but in Mindy's half. That would leave Amber with the dentist and the septic tank man.

She shook her head, determined to keep the vet

and the Secret Service agent. "No, that wouldn't work. Where would we draw the line? In the middle of our houses? That would be dumb."

"It would not," Mindy flared. "You're just saying that because you want to keep the good people on *your* side."

Amber got mad, too. "Well, if you're so smart, why don't you just keep the whole street? I'll go find my *own* neighborhood."

"Go ahead. See if I care!"

Amber leafed angrily through her magazine. It was all Delight's fault. Everything that had happened this whole rotten day was Delight's fault.

She cut out two pictures. One showed a man typing at a computer. He could represent any of the fathers on her block who worked in an office. The other showed an Eskimo digging a hole in a snowbank. Amber thought he could be the septic tank man. That's what septic tank men did all the time, dig holes. Then she remembered she wasn't doing her report on Carriage Street. Mindy was. Amber had to find her own neighborhood.

"Here," she said, slapping the Eskimo picture on Mindy's desk. "You might as well have this."

Mindy smacked the picture back on Amber's desk. "I don't want it. I have my own pictures."

"This is the septic tank man!" Amber hissed.

"Mr. Potts is not an Eskimo."

"That doesn't matter! It could be him in the wintertime. Can't you ever think of anything by yourself?" As soon as the words were out, Amber was sorry she said them.

Mindy's reply was as frosty as the snowbank in the photograph. "Yes, I can. I think I don't want you for a friend anymore."

"Fine with me!" Amber retorted, forgetting to keep her voice down.

At that moment, Mrs. Sharp swooped down on them like a crow landing in a cornfield. "Amber, you have disturbed the class once too often today. Take your things and go to the corner."

Amber's stomach twisted. Not the time-out corner! When you sat there, everyone in class knew you were in trouble.

"Come on, Amber." Mrs. Sharp gathered Amber's magazine and paper and took them to the time-out desk.

With dragging feet, Amber trudged to the lone desk pulled up close to the blackboard. Her face burned with shame. Ms. Lovejoy had never treated her like this.

She glanced over her shoulder and saw Delight Wakefield staring at her. Amber turned quickly around. This was Delight's fault, too, she figured. Delight had put Amber in a bad mood, which caused her to fight with Mindy.

"Let's finish up social studies," Mrs. Sharp said. "It's time for handwriting." She passed out their green cursive workbooks.

Amber was lonely in her corner. She felt like the moon of a distant planet. Everybody down on the planet was having fun. Nobody cared that she was up in the cold sky, by herself.

"We're going to write letters." Mrs. Sharp went to the board and began writing in her perfect, loopy cursive. *Dear Mother, Today we are learning how to write a letter. I hope I write it well. Yours very truly,*

Mrs. Sharp told them where to put the date, the greeting, and the closing. "Copy the letter on the board for practice. Then I want you to write your own letter."

Amber hurriedly copied the "Dear Mother" letter in sloppy cursive. She was anxious to write another letter, to Mindy.

Dear Mindy, Im sorry we had a fight. Im not mad. Are you? Yours very truly, Amber.

She folded the paper into a tight square and waited until Mrs. Sharp bent over Henry's desk to answer a question. Leaning back, Amber hurled the note in the direction of Mindy's desk. It missed and bounced off Carly's desk instead.

Of course Mrs. Sharp saw the flying paper. She marched over and picked it up. Without reading it, she gave Amber a stern look.

"I did not tell you to write a note, Amber. I asked you to write a formal letter. What happens when we throw papers in class?"

"She has to write sentences!" Delight offered.

"I asked Amber."

"I have to write sentences?" Amber replied in a small voice.

"Exactly. 'I will not throw papers in class.' Twenty-five times. After you complete your letter."

Amber couldn't remember when she'd had such a terrible day. First, everybody brought their stuffed animals and nobody noticed her raccoon. Then Mrs. Sharp took R.C. away. Then she and Mindy had a fight and Amber had to sit in the time-out corner. *Now* she had to write sentences. It was too much.

Third grade wasn't worth it, she decided glumly.

None of these awful things had happened in second grade. If only she could go back to last year.

Maybe she *could*. Anything was possible.

She thought a moment. Then in her best cursive, she wrote, *Dear Mrs. Sharp, I dont like third grade anymore. Im quiting. Im going back to Ms. Lovejoys room. Yours very truly, Amber Gillian Cantrell.*

Amber laid the letter on the corner of her desk. Mrs. Sharp would be by shortly to pick it up. Her teacher would be shocked to learn Amber was quitting third grade. But Amber had made up her mind.

Chapter
SIX

Mrs. Sharp did not make a fuss when she read Amber's letter. Amber was surprised. She thought her teacher would beg her to stay or at least ask Amber to reconsider. That just proved that her teacher didn't care whether Amber was in her class or not.

"So you are resigning," Mrs. Sharp said calmly. "I'm sorry to hear you are unhappy in third grade." To the other students she said, "I have to speak to another teacher down the hall. Continue working quietly on your letters."

Mrs. Sharp left the room. Amber hoped she was going to talk to Ms. Lovejoy. When Mrs. Sharp returned a few moments later, she informed Amber she could leave Room Six. "Ms. Lovejoy says she will be delighted to have you back in her class. You may report there after lunch."

Amber couldn't wait to tell her astonishing news to Mindy, but Mindy was still mad at her.

At lunchtime, Amber sidled next to Mindy in the line to go down to the cafeteria.

Mindy kept her face turned stonily away.

"You'll be sorry when I'm gone," Amber said meaningfully.

She made her announcement at the lunch table. Mindy was sitting at the other end with Delight and Carly. Lisa sat in Mindy's old chair across from Amber.

"I quit third grade," Amber declared, loud enough for Mindy to hear.

"Good," said Henry. "Why don't you quit the world while you're at it?" He and David cracked up.

"I'm not kidding," Amber said. "I quit. I wrote a letter to Mrs. Sharp."

"Why?" Lisa demanded. "Why did you quit?"

Carly answered before Amber could. "Because Amber and Mindy had a big fight, that's why."

"That has nothing to do with it. I don't like third grade anymore," Amber said airily. "I'm going to Ms. Lovejoy's room."

Lisa stopped picking raisins out of her muffin. "But that's second grade! Amber, are you crazy? You'll be with *babies*! Second- *and* first-graders!"

"I don't care. Anything is better than third grade.

I hate it," Amber said, biting defiantly into her sandwich.

"You'll have to go to third grade next year," Lisa pointed out.

Amber hadn't thought of that possibility. She only wanted the blissful warmth of Ms. Lovejoy's smile. She wanted to be where there was no Delight Wakefield, showing her up at every turn.

"Mrs. Sharp doesn't like me," she said. "And I don't like her. So I'm going back to second grade."

"You can't stay in second grade all your life," David said.

Deep down, Amber knew she couldn't. Maybe she could stay in second grade until Mrs. Sharp retired. After all, her teacher wasn't young. Not with black-and-gray hair. Her teaching days were probably numbered.

Or maybe Amber could skip third grade altogether and go directly to fourth. It had happened before. There was a boy in Justin's class who was too smart for sixth grade, so they promoted him to seventh, just like that.

Everyone thought she was crazy to go back to second grade. Mindy, whose opinion mattered most to Amber, didn't say anything.

At least she wouldn't have to sit next to an ex-best friend anymore. In Ms. Lovejoy's room, she could start over, make new friends.

After lunch, Amber packed her things. When her desk was cleared, she stood up. "I'm leaving now."

Mrs. Sharp was checking math homework. The rest of the class worked on multiplication.

"Good-bye, Amber. Good luck," was all Mrs. Sharp said.

Without a backward glance, Amber left Room Six forever. She walked purposefully down the hall to Ms. Lovejoy's room.

"Amber, hello!" Ms. Lovejoy welcomed her. "We were just about to have our mid-afternoon march."

Amber bounced happily into her old room. She remembered how Ms. Lovejoy let her class march around once or twice a day, "to get the kinks out." In Mrs. Sharp's room, you stayed at your desk.

"We have a new student," Ms. Lovejoy told the class. "This is Amber Cantrell. She's going to be in our room now. Let's greet Amber with our best Virginia Run manners."

The little kids gaped at her, without any shred of manners. Amber wanted to sit down, so she wouldn't feel like such a stranger.

She looked around for her old desk. There it was, in the middle row. A little boy with red hair was sitting in it.

"That boy," Amber whispered to Ms. Lovejoy. "He's sitting in my desk. Isn't that where I'm going to sit?"

Her teacher shook her head. "I'm sorry, but as you see, your old desk is occupied. Ben has been there all month. It would be unfair to make him move now."

"Then where am I going to sit?" Amber scanned the rows of desks. The second-grade side of the room appeared to be full.

"I've got a nice desk for you over here." Ms. Lovejoy led Amber to the *first-grade* side of the classroom. A low table with a small chair, the furniture the babies used, stood empty.

"B-but, Ms. Lovejoy," Amber stammered. "I'm not a first-grader. I'm supposed to get a real desk."

"I'm sorry, Amber, but this is the only desk I have available." She smiled her familiar warm smile. "You'll have plenty of room to spread out your things. And you have two nice neighbors, Gary and Shannon."

Gary grinned at her. He was missing one of his front teeth and reminded Amber of a jack-o'-lantern. The girl called Shannon stuck out her tongue at Amber. Amber certainly did not want first-graders for friends.

Ms. Lovejoy clapped her hands. "Time to march, everybody. Let's wake up and stretch!"

The class marched in a snaky line around the room. Students raised their arms and stamped their feet. Amber enjoyed the chance to make noise. She noticed that she was taller than the other kids. A lot taller.

When she sat down at her seat after the march, her knees banged the bottom of the table.

"You don't fit," Gary observed.

Shannon asked rudely, "Hey, big kid. How come you're in here? Are you dumb?"

"No, I'm not dumb," Amber said. "I'm very smart." But she couldn't explain what was so smart about going backward.

Ms. Lovejoy passed out pictures of autumn leaves for the first-graders to color.

"How come *she* didn't get one?" Shannon asked the teacher.

"Because," Amber said smugly, "I get *real* work."

A few moments later, Ms. Lovejoy handed Amber a sheet of arithmetic problems. It was all addition. Easy addition, like five plus seven. No double numbers.

"Ms. Lovejoy," Amber said. "I had this stuff last year. A long time ago."

"I know that, dear," her teacher replied. "But this is what my second-graders are working on now. Remember, you're a second-grader, too. You have to do what the rest of my class does."

"Okay." Amber sighed and looked at the worksheet with dismay. It would take her about three seconds to finish the problems. In Mrs. Sharp's class, they were working on multiplication. Amber liked multiplication. It was neat the way she could arrive at the answer fast, without having to add up long columns of numbers.

Gary glanced over at her paper. "That looks hard."

"It isn't, really." Not when you've had it twice, she thought morosely. She peeked at the maple leaf Gary was coloring a dreary brown. He had trouble staying in the lines. Feeling generous, Amber said, "Here. I'll show you a trick."

She lined up all his crayons, then lightly skimmed a blue crayon over the design.

Shannon watched intently. "Blue! Who ever heard of a blue leaf? No wonder they sent you back here."

"I wasn't sent back. I *came* back," Amber corrected. "What you do is use all your crayons, but don't press down, okay?"

Gary eagerly obeyed. When he held up his multicolored leaf picture, Amber felt as proud as he did.

"Ms. Lovejoy," Shannon cried. "I want another leaf picture so I can make one like Gary's."

The bell rang. The students on the second-grade side of the room scrambled for the door. It was their recess period. They went outside to join the other second-grade classes.

Amber rose to join them.

"Where are you going?" Gary shrieked.

"Outside. It's recess."

"I don't want you to go!" His bottom lip pushed out.

"Neither do I!" Shannon chimed in. She had changed her mind about Amber after the art lesson.

Amber blinked uncertainly at Ms. Lovejoy. She wanted to go outside but she didn't want to leave Gary and Shannon crying.

"I'll stay inside," she muttered. Her new "neighbors" cheered.

The first-graders had already had their recess earlier in the day. It was time for them to go to art.

"Please line up," Ms. Lovejoy said. The first-graders scrambled to form a line.

Amber remained seated. She wanted to sit at her desk and read.

"Hey, Amber!" Gary yelled. "I saved you a place!"

"Me too!" shrilled Shannon, not about to be outdone.

"We're going to be quiet when we go down to Mrs. Chandler's art room," Ms. Lovejoy chided gently.

"I'm not going until Amber comes," said Gary.

With a sigh, Amber realized she had no choice. She put her book away and got into line, between Gary and Shannon. They walked down the hall to the art room, where Ms. Lovejoy left them with a little wave.

Mrs. Chandler, the art teacher, seemed surprised to see Amber with the first-graders, but didn't make a fuss. Gary and Shannon pulled Amber over to their table, which was covered with a big sheet of paper. Mrs. Chandler set pots of finger-paints on each table and gave them each an old shirt to put on over their clothes.

"Let's be creative," she told the class. "Paint anything you like, just don't paint each other. Keep the paint on the paper, please!"

The little kids dove into the paint pots, smearing streaks of orange and green and blue in wild swoops. Gary made red squiggles on his side of the paper.

"I'm a snake," he said to Shannon. She shrieked as Gary's snake wriggled across the neat brown house she was painting.

"Hey, Amber," Gary said. "Aren't you going to paint?"

Normally Amber loved art class, because she enjoyed making things. But finger-painting was for babies. She didn't like making messy, pointless pictures.

She had made a big mistake.

Nothing was the way it had been last year. She didn't have her old desk. Classwork was boring. She shouldn't have come back.

She took off her painting shirt and quickly left the room. Back in Ms. Lovejoy's class, she found the teacher marking papers. She looked up when Amber came in.

"Amber, is something wrong?"

"Ms. Lovejoy, can I talk to you?"

Ms. Lovejoy put down her pen. "Of course."

Amber didn't know how to begin without hurting her teacher's feelings. After all, Amber had asked Ms. Lovejoy to take her back.

Her teacher seemed to understand. "It's not what you hoped it would be, is it? Coming back to my class, I mean."

"No," Amber confessed. "I thought it would be like last year. But that's not your fault," she added hastily.

"I'm sorry you're disappointed."

"I feel so dumb. Gary was right. I don't fit." Amber hung her head.

"You mustn't blame yourself. Adjusting to a new situation can be very difficult sometimes." Ms. Lovejoy took off the wire-rimmed glasses she used for reading. "When I was in ninth grade, I didn't get along with one of my teachers."

Amber glanced up, amazed. Perfect Ms. Lovejoy in trouble! "What happened?"

"I was so unhappy, I actually called my old eighth-grade teacher, at the junior high school. She was my favorite teacher and I knew she'd help me." Ms. Lovejoy looked down at her hands, folded neatly over the pen. "My old teacher urged me to try to work it out. Then she said she had to get back to her class. I realized my old teacher had new students. I wasn't in her class anymore. I had moved on, whether I wanted to or not."

"Did you ever like that other teacher?"

Ms. Lovejoy gave a rueful smile. "Well, we weren't exactly friends, but we did make it through the year. You see, Amber, there are times in our lives when we are not ready to move forward, but we can't go backward, either."

Amber knew what Ms. Lovejoy was trying to tell her. She would have to go back to Mrs. Sharp's class.

"Can't I go to fourth grade instead?" she pleaded. "I already know my multiplication tables."

"You don't want to skip third grade. It'll be one of the best years of your life."

Amber doubted it.

"Would you like to stay here the rest of the day?" Ms. Lovejoy offered.

Amber was tempted. Maybe if she didn't go back to Mrs. Sharp's room until tomorrow, everyone would have forgotten she had quit third grade. But she would have to go back to the art room and finger-paint with the little kids.

"No," she said. "I'll go back now."

"It'll be okay, Amber. Just give it a little time." Ms. Lovejoy hugged her. "I'll help you pack your things."

At the door, Amber hesitated. Her old teacher waved good-bye. Amber waved back, then walked heavily up the hall to Room Six.

Mrs. Sharp was reading a story to the class.

Amber wasn't sure how to enter the room. She waited until Mrs. Sharp turned a page, then announced, "Well. I'm back."

The other kids looked at her with mild interest, as if she'd just returned from the nurse's office.

Mrs. Sharp paused, one fingertip holding her place in the book. "We're glad you're back, Amber. Take your seat, please."

Amber settled into her old desk, pleased it was the right size. She glanced over at Mindy, but Mindy faced the front, evidently still mad at Amber.

Amber wasn't worried. Now that she was back, she'd win Mindy over again. After all, they were best friends.

Mrs. Sharp continued with the story. She wasn't a good reader, not like Ms. Lovejoy, who changed her voice to fit each character in the story. But the story was about King Arthur and sounded neat. It was not the kind of story she would have heard in second grade.

Amber leaned forward, her chin on her fists, eager to listen. Then she noticed the red button on the corner of her desk. She checked her backpack. No, her "R.C. and P." button was still securely pinned to the flap.

It must be Mindy's button. She probably didn't realize she had lost it.

"You dropped this," Amber whispered, anxious for a chance to make up. She put the button on Mindy's desk.

Mindy pushed it back. "I didn't drop it."

"What do you mean? Don't you want it?"

Mindy whispered so Mrs. Sharp wouldn't overhear. "If you can quit third grade, Amber Cantrell, then I can quit our club."

Amber was stunned. Without Mindy, there wasn't any club. She couldn't be in a club by herself.

Feeling someone's stare, she looked up and met Delight Wakefield's eyes. Now she knew why Mindy gave back the button.

Her best friend was in Delight's club now.

Chapter
SEVEN

On the ride home that day, Amber was more miserable than ever. Nobody paid Amber any attention at all. It was as if she were invisible.

Amber sat with Mindy, although Mindy had been slow to move over for Amber. Mindy seemed to find the view outside fascinating. Amber looked too, but saw only the same old houses and shopping centers.

The bus ahead of theirs, carrying the kids who lived in Mockingbird Ridge, turned off onto the first side street. Kids from Amber's bus yelled out the windows at the Mockingbird Ridge kids. Amber wished she had enough nerve to lean out of her window and jeer at Delight Wakefield, who was somewhere on that bus. If it weren't for Delight, she and Mindy would still be best friends. Now they weren't even speaking.

The worst was yet to come.

Amber had to go to Mindy's house until her mother came home from the shop.

As the bus bounced over the bridge into Creekside, she wondered if she could pretend she was sick. If she told Mindy's mother she had something contagious, like malaria, she'd be sent home. She tried to recall a movie about a man lost in Africa who had malaria. He shivered and sweated from fever and said things that didn't make sense. That might work, she decided. Mindy's mother would be so concerned, she'd call Amber's mother and tell her to come home right away.

The bus stopped at the corner of Carriage and Buggy Whip. Amber climbed off after Mindy and followed her into the house.

A solid wall of Sarah's wails met them at the door.

Karen ran to greet them, wearing a towel draped around her shoulders like a cape and an old red bathing suit over her pants and shirt.

"Sarah's crying again," she announced. "Mommy's grouchy. Guess who I am? Woman-Woman!"

"Woman-Woman?" Amber asked. "Who's that?"

Mindy put her backpack on the kitchen chair. "She means Wonder Woman. It's Karen's favorite program."

This was the first thing Mindy had said since she declared she was quitting the club. Believing Mindy was offering her a crumb of their old friendship, Amber said cheerfully, "Oh, that old TV show. I haven't watched it in ages. It's pretty good sometimes. Do you want to watch it?"

Mindy was dialing the wall phone and didn't answer. "Is Delight there?" she said into the receiver.

Amber felt an icy chill. Mindy was calling Delight, right in front of her! Delight must have come on the phone, because Mindy turned away, suddenly secretive, and practically whispered into the receiver. Amber heard Mindy ask Delight if she could come over. The chill made her shiver. She wouldn't have to pretend she was sick. She really *was*.

Karen twirled into the kitchen. "Who's gonna watch Woman-Woman with me?"

"Not me. I'm busy," Mindy answered, hanging up.

Karen appealed to Amber. "Will you watch it with me?"

Just then Mrs. Alexander came in. She looked exhausted.

"Do not make a sound," she cautioned. "I finally got Sarah to sleep." Amber realized the wailing had stopped. "It's a nice day. Why don't you girls play outside? Take Karen, please. She's been waiting all afternoon for you to come home."

"Aww, Mom," Mindy complained. "Delight's

79

coming over. We're going to work on our social studies project. I don't want Karen tagging along."

"Can't she go with you?" Mrs. Alexander asked.

"We're supposed to go to people's houses and talk to them. We can't take a four-year-old with us. She'd just be in the way."

Karen swung on the back of a chair, waiting to see who would win, her big sister or her mother.

"What I wouldn't give for a half hour of peace and quiet," Mrs. Alexander said wearily. "All right. I'll entertain Karen while you girls do your project."

Mindy glanced at Amber. Amber knew Mindy was thinking that *she'd* just be in the way too. Mindy had not said a word about Amber joining them to work on the project.

Now was the right time to go into her malaria act. She wanted to be sent home *before* Delight got to Mindy's house.

It was too late to sweat. Amber had planned to splash water on her face and get her hair wet. But she could still shiver and talk nonsense.

"The moon is in the bathtub," she mumbled, shaking from head to foot.

"What did you say, Amber?" Mrs. Alexander was shoulder-deep in the refrigerator, getting the girls some juice.

Mindy stared at her as if she'd lost her mind.

Amber knew she couldn't keep up the act. She

would just have to stick it out until her mother came home. "I said, I'll play with Karen," she offered limply.

Mrs. Alexander handed them each a brownie on a paper napkin. "Don't you have to work on your social studies project too?"

"I don't have a neighborhood," Amber told her. "I have to find one first. I don't mind playing with Karen. Really."

"You're an angel." Mrs. Alexander gave her a swift hug, then went to lie down before supper.

"You don't have to find another neighborhood," Mindy said to Amber as they ate their brownies.

Amber's hopes took wing again. Was Mindy inviting her to go with them after all?

"I don't?" she said, her voice lifting.

"No. See, Delight figured out she lived on the same side of Carriage Street as me. So we're doing this side of Carriage together. You can have your half of the street back."

Amber let Mindy's words sink in. She was still not included.

A knock sounded at the door. Mindy ran to open it. Delight came in. Her magnificent hair was pulled up in a ponytail.

"Hi, Amber," she said. "Is that your little sister?" she asked Mindy.

"Yeah, that's Karen. My other little sister is sleeping."

"I like your hair," Karen said, suddenly shy.

Delight smiled at her. "Thanks."

"Want a brownie?" Mindy asked Delight. Amber was beginning to feel like a fifth wheel.

Delight shook her head, clutching her notebook. "I'm kind of nervous about this project. I'm glad you're doing it with me, Mindy."

"Why?" Amber blurted. "I mean, why are you nervous?" Surely the world-traveler didn't have anything to be afraid of.

"I don't know the people on my street yet," Delight replied. "We just moved here, you know."

"But you've lived all over the world," Amber argued. "You can talk to people in French and Japanese."

"I can only speak a few words of Japanese," Delight said. "Anyway, there aren't any Japanese people on my street. Or any French ones either. Sometimes it's hard when you move to a new place..." She let the sentence trail away.

Mindy unzipped her backpack and took out her own notebook. "We'd better get going, Delight. We'll start in your neighborhood, if you want. I know everybody on my street."

They went out the door, giggling and chattering. Amber stood in the kitchen until Karen tugged at her sleeve.

"You promised to watch Woman-Woman with me,

Amber. It's almost over." Then the little girl added, "I like your hair, too."

Amber was glad *somebody* still liked her. She watched the rest of Karen's program and then they played Candyland until Amber's mother pulled into the driveway. Amber went home, glad the next day was Wednesday. She wouldn't have to go to Mindy's house after school until Thursday. Maybe by then she could convince her mother she was old enough to stay home by herself.

"This is about Parents' Night." Amber handed her mother the announcement from school.

It was Friday evening, at last. Amber had not been able to convince her mother she was old enough to stay by herself after school and had gone, with heavy heart, to Mindy's house on Thursday and today. Mindy and Delight had worked on their social studies project both afternoons. Amber had started her own project, interviewing the few people who were home on her side of the street. She'd taken Karen with her. She didn't mind Mindy's little sister, and it was nice to have some company.

"Parents' Night already?" Mrs. Cantrell remarked, looking over the flyer. "It seems like yesterday was the first day of school. I can't believe you've been in school a whole month."

Amber felt like she'd been in third grade her

whole life. "Our class will be in the assembly," she said. "Do you think Dad will come?"

"I don't know, honey. I'm sure he'd like to. His schedule is pretty hectic these days." Noting Amber's downcast expression, her mother added, "Why don't we call him and see if he has plans a week from Thursday? I need to find out when he's coming tomorrow anyway."

Her mother dialed the number, spoke a few words to Amber's father, then handed the phone to Amber.

"Daddy? Are we going to the Smithsonian tomorrow?" Her father had promised last weekend, when he had to cancel their plans, that he would take them to the museum.

"We sure are," her father replied. It was nice to hear his voice.

"Daddy, Parents' Night is a week from Thursday. My class is going to be in the program. Can you come?"

"I'm not sure, Pumpkin. Let me check my schedule. I should know by the beginning of the week. Are you going to be the star?" he teased.

"I don't know. We haven't decided what we're going to do yet." Amber wrapped the phone cord around her wrist. Last year she had sort of been the star, when Ms. Lovejoy let her stand in the front row and hold her raccoon.

"I'll see you tomorrow by nine. Tell Justin to be

ready this time."

"I will." She hung up, remembering the girl her father had told her about, the one in his third-grade class. Julie, the ball of fire, who had starred in her father's class play. She wondered what kind of program her class would perform in the assembly. Would there be a spot for a star?

Mrs. Sharp brought up the subject of Parents' Night first thing on Monday, before they began social studies.

"You took home flyers about Parents' Night last Friday. I hope all your parents will visit Virginia Run Elementary. I am eager to meet them and discuss your work."

Henry Hoffstedder groaned. Mrs. Sharp silenced him with a look. Amber knew why Henry didn't want his parents to come. He hardly ever did any work in class.

"As you know, our class has the honor of being in the assembly. I would like to talk about what kind of program we could do. Put on a skit...sing...it's up to you."

"Let's do a monster program!" David suggested. The other boys instantly agreed, making monster sounds.

"The program," Mrs. Sharp explained, "must relate to what we've been learning in class. Your parents want to see what you've been learning this year so far."

"Mine would rather see monsters," Henry muttered.

Amber thought Henry's parents were used to seeing monsters, having him around. She started to nudge Mindy and share this joke with her, but then remembered she and Mindy weren't friends anymore.

"Any other suggestions? Does anybody have an idea?"

Delight Wakefield raised her hand. "How about something to do with other countries? You know, like they are our neighbors?"

"Excellent." Mrs. Sharp wrote *Other People, Other Lands* on the blackboard. "A very good suggestion, Delight. This ties in nicely with our neighborhood project and gives all of you a chance to participate. We could be a parade of countries."

"My parents have lots of stuff from the places they've been to," Delight went on. "Hats and scarves and things. I know my mother would let me bring them in for us to use."

"Wonderful," Mrs. Sharp gushed. "Each of you could carry an object from a different country, or wear a piece of native clothing. You could step forward and say a few words about what country you represent."

Delight wouldn't stop talking. "I have a costume

from Japan, Mrs. Sharp! A kimono. You should see it—it's blue silk and has this hatlike thing. I can wear that!"

Amber couldn't stand it. Delight's idea was accepted before anyone else got to say a word, not counting David's dumb idea. Delight's idea was even dumber. Amber did not want to stand on stage holding a scarf, especially if Delight Wakefield was going to wear a whole costume. That would make Delight the star!

"Mrs. Sharp!" she burst out without raising her hand.

For once the teacher didn't reprimand her. "Yes, Amber. What is it?"

Now that everyone was looking at her, she wished she hadn't spoken up.

"Amber, do you have a suggestion for the assembly?" Mrs. Sharp urged.

If only she could think of an idea! Last summer, when she and Mindy were having so much fun with their stuffed animals, Amber thought of new ideas every day. But now her brain seemed dried up.

"Do you have something to say?" Mrs. Sharp asked.

"No," she said meekly. "I just thought...maybe somebody else might have another idea."

The teacher looked around at the class. "Does anyone else have any ideas for the assembly?"

No one did.

"All right. Room Six will put on an international parade."

It was decided. They would all be on the stage during the assembly, but Delight Wakefield would be the star.

Amber clenched her fists under her desk. It wasn't fair. Delight already had the prettiest name and the longest hair. Did she have to be the star, too?

EIGHT

Rain droned against the windowpanes, matching Mrs. Sharp's tone as she reviewed the social studies chapter with the class.

Amber gazed out of the window, her mood as gloomy as the weather. Indoor recess again today. She hated indoor recess.

Yesterday, when the weather turned rotten, Room Six had crowded into the gym with the other third-grade classes. The gym smelled like wet shoes and old lunch bags. Instead of playing fun games, they had to do folk dancing. David Jackson was Amber's reluctant partner. He stomped around the circle, refusing to touch her because he said her hands felt icky.

Amber wished she could tell Mindy what David had said to her. That was the worst part about not being best friends anymore. She only had R.C. to tell her thoughts to.

If she and Mindy had had an ordinary fight, they would have made up by now. But the problem between them wasn't a fight. It was Delight. If only she had stayed in Japan, Amber thought glumly. If only her parents had bought a house anyplace besides Carriage Street.

"In a neighborhood," Mrs. Sharp was saying, "people learn to live and work together. They respect each other's feelings."

Delight Wakefield certainly didn't respect Amber's feelings or she wouldn't have stolen her best friend, Amber thought. She doodled in her notebook, then began scribbling a pretend letter from her raccoon.

"People respect each other's privacy in a neighborhood," Mrs. Sharp went on. "They respect each other's property—a person's house and yard are considered his space."

Amber wrote: *Dear Pearl, Are you still mad? Im not mad if your not mad. I want to be freinds agin. I miss you alot. Your freind, R.C.*

She listened absently to the teacher as she drew a sad raccoon.

"This classroom is like a neighborhood. Think of your desk as your house. The person next to you is your next-door neighbor and the other desks around you make up your neighborhood. You have learned to respect other people's belongings. Carly, would you take a pencil off Henry's desk?"

Not unless she wanted to get cooties, Amber thought.

"Not without asking him," Carly replied.

"That's right. Carly respects Henry's property. You also learn to respect other people's feelings. Lisa, if you accidently shoved Mindy on the playground, what would you say?"

Next to Amber, Mindy giggled.

"I'd tell Mindy I was sorry," Lisa said. "And I'd see if she needed to go to the nurse."

"Very good. Are there any questions? Henry?"

"Suppose you don't like somebody," Henry said. "I mean, really, *really* don't like somebody in your neighborhood. Should you move or make the other guy move?"

Mrs. Sharp leaned against her desk. "That's a good question, Henry. It happens more often than you think. It's hard to like everyone. Some people aren't very likeable. But even if you can't be friends with that person, you must learn to get along with him. You can't have a fistfight every time you meet."

This remark brought laughter. Henry punched out an invisible opponent. Mrs. Sharp laughed along with the class.

"Does anyone have anything to add to this discussion? Yes, Delight?"

Amber was drawing a border of broken hearts around R.C.'s letter. She looked up when Delight began speaking in a soft, tentative voice.

"About what Henry said about moving. I know a lot about it. We move almost every year." Her tone sounded wistful.

Mrs. Sharp nodded as if she understood. "Tell the class what it is like to move and be the new person in the neighborhood."

"It's really hard," Delight replied. "Going to new schools...meeting new kids. I was always different. Other kids called me 'the American.'"

"And how did that make you feel?" Mrs. Sharp encouraged her.

"Like I didn't belong. I don't like moving around. You should try to stay in the same place and get along, like you said. Even if all the people aren't very nice." Delight ducked her head, letting a honey-colored curtain of hair hide her face.

Amber couldn't believe her ears. She thought Delight had a great life moving from country to country. Maybe it wasn't so great, after all.

The last bell of the day rang. Mindy packed her books in her pink backpack and left her desk the same time Amber left hers. Their eyes met briefly. Then Mindy ran ahead to catch up to Delight.

"Are you coming over?" Mindy asked Delight. "We can make jewelry. I bought some new beads last night."

Amber pushed past them and trudged out the door. It was Wednesday, so she could go straight home. At least she wouldn't have to watch her ex-best friend and her worst enemy having fun.

"You haven't told me much about the play you're doing for Parents' Night," Mrs. Cantrell said.

Amber cut out a square from a plastic garbage bag. She was making a rain slicker for R.C. "We're having our first rehearsal tomorrow. I don't really know what I'm doing yet." She didn't want to admit she would only be on stage a few seconds and that Delight Wakefield was the star.

"Well, I'm sure it'll be entertaining," Mrs. Cantrell said. She carefully folded the quilt she had recently finished repairing and slipped it into a cloth sack. Amber knew the good-as-new quilt would be displayed in the window of her mother's shop tomorrow.

Her mother glanced around the messy kitchen. "Who left all these dishes?"

"Justin," Amber was happy to say.

"Justin!"

Amber's brother came in from the den, a half-empty bag of Doritos dangling from one hand. "Yeah?" he said.

"What have I told you about cleaning up after yourself?" Mrs. Cantrell said. "Everybody pulls their own weight around here or this family will sink. Now clean up that mess."

Grudgingly, Justin rinsed his dirty dishes with cold water. "You're supposed to use hot water," Amber pointed out.

"You're supposed to mind your own business."

"Stop it, you two," Mrs. Cantrell said mildly. "Amber, I talked to Mindy's mom today. She wondered if I knew why you and Mindy weren't getting along. It seems Mindy plays with another girl after school now. She said this girl has the longest hair she's ever seen on a child."

"Delight," Amber mumbled miserably. "That new girl I told you about."

"Oh, that one! I see..." Her mother patted Amber's arm. "You and Mindy will work it out. You've been friends too long to let anything hurt that friendship."

It didn't matter how long they'd been friends, Amber decided. Mindy liked Delight better and that was that.

"I forgot to tell you, Dad called." Justin slopped the dish rag around on the counter, scattering crumbs.

"What did he want?" Mrs. Cantrell asked. "Don't tell me he's cancelling this weekend?"

"No, he just said he couldn't go to Amber's school thing next Thursday."

Amber leaped up from the table. "He did not! You're making it up, Justin Cantrell!"

Her brother laughed at her fury. "He did too. I'm not lying. His exact words were, 'I'm not a hundred percent sure, but I don't think I'll make it to Amber's school next Thursday night.' Call him and ask him yourself, if you don't believe me."

"Mom," Amber cried. "He said he'd come to Parents' Night!"

"Amber, it's still over a week away. He might be able to come. Don't write him off yet."

"I'm going outside." Amber bundled R.C. in the new rain slicker and put on her own raincoat.

The rain had slowed to a drizzle. Amber walked down Carriage Street, her head down. She knew why her father wasn't coming to Parents' Night. Somehow he'd found out that Amber wasn't the star. He didn't want to bother if his daughter wasn't like that ball of fire Julie. Amber figured Delight was a lot like that girl in her father's old class.

Mindy and Delight were probably having a great time at Mindy's house. She and Delight were best friends now. Amber didn't have anybody.

When she reached the bridge over Rocky Run, she stopped to lean over the rail. The beaver dam had a huge hole in it. Muddy creek water, swollen from the rains, gushed over the dam.

Amber wondered what the beavers would do now.

She started to throw twigs into the creek to help them rebuild their dam. But it seemed useless. It would take more than a few sticks to fix that big hole.

"David, how many times do I have to tell you those chopsticks are not drumsticks? If I catch you using Henry's head as a drum again, you're going to the office."

In the echoing auditorium, Mrs. Sharp's voice rang with more authority than ever.

David put the chopsticks down.

"All right. Let's line up again. A neat circle, please."

They were rehearsing the Parents' Night program for the last time. The assembly was tomorrow night. Ms. Lovejoy's class was rehearsing, too. They were doing the same Big Forest play Amber was in last year. First- and second-graders jumped around the aisles, wearing brown paper "tree" costumes they kept tearing. Ms. Lovejoy had to stop every two minutes and Scotch-tape somebody's leaves.

At least Amber's class had real props. Delight brought in a huge box filled with objects from other countries. She was in the little dressing area offstage, changing into her Japanese costume. Delight was the only one with a complete outfit.

"Lisa, you're first, remember," Mrs. Sharp said. "Step to the front and announce your country. Be sure to hold your tray up so everyone can see it. Then step back into the circle." She punched the cassette recorder. Piano music began to play.

The third-graders marched in time to the music. At Mrs. Sharp's signal, Lisa stepped out of the line, faced the imaginary audience, and chirped, "I'm Afghanistan!" as she held up a brass tray. Each student carried an object representing a different country.

Amber was Turkey. She carried gold brocade slippers that curled up at the toes. She was going to feel stupid saying, "I'm Turkey" and holding up a pair of slippers in front of all those parents tomorrow night. If only she had a better country.

Mindy was France. She carried Delight's stuffed dog, Row-bear. The only reason Mindy got to carry the dog, Amber figured, was because she was Delight's new best friend.

"I'm China!" David yelled, brandishing the chopsticks like swords.

It was Amber's turn. "I'm Turkey," she mumbled, dropping one of the slippers.

"Speak up!" Mrs. Sharp commanded. "Amber, hold on to the slippers properly."

"Butterfingers," sneered Henry, who was right behind Amber as "Germany." Amber wanted to knock that silly hat with the feather in the band right off his head.

The second time they marched around, Amber forgot to step out of the line. She wasn't the only one making mistakes. Lisa couldn't say "Afghanistan." She called it "Africa-stan."

"Let's take a break," Mrs. Sharp finally said.

Amber rushed away from the group and walked over to where Ms. Lovejoy was cutting out more brown paper "leaves" at a card table. She wished the assembly was over with. Maybe her old teacher would put her in a better mood.

"Hello, Amber," Ms. Lovejoy said. "Your pageant is going very well."

"It's okay. Except my part is dumb."

"Every role in a program is important," Ms. Lovejoy said.

Amber didn't want to talk about the pageant. "Your class is doing the Big Forest, isn't it?"

"You remember that from last year?" She smiled at her students, who were hopping around down front. "I'm afraid they make better Mexican jumping beans than oak trees. Where's Mindy? I haven't seen you two together lately."

Amber picked up a pair of scissors and idly opened and closed the blades. "Oh...we had a fight."

"Oh, dear." Ms. Lovejoy gave a sympathetic cluck. "Can't you patch it up? It would be a shame to ruin a wonderful friendship over an argument."

Amber didn't mention that Mindy had traded best friends.

Just then one of the first-graders fell down and began to howl. Ms. Lovejoy ran over to comfort the little girl.

"My class, let's take our places," Mrs. Sharp ordered.

Amber didn't move. She couldn't stand the thought of parading around the stage one more time, carrying those dumb slippers.

The door to the dressing room opened and Delight stepped on stage.

"Wow!" David exclaimed. "Look at Delight!"

Delight's costume was turquoise-blue silk with pink flowers embroidered all over it. The skirt touched her ankles and a wide pink sash went around her middle. She wore wooden sandals that she couldn't walk in very well. A little hat made of silk cherry blossoms and tassels was perched on her head.

Delight looked like a girl in a travel program, Amber thought with envy. She would steal the show for sure. Nobody would look at Amber with her stupid slippers. All eyes would be on Delight Wakefield.

Amber wasn't the only girl who was envious. "How come she gets to wear a whole outfit?" asked Carly. "The rest of us only have things to carry."

"Because it's Delight's costume," Mrs. Sharp replied. "We should be very grateful her parents are letting us use these things."

Delight stumbled over to Mrs. Sharp. "I can't get the headpiece on right. My mother says she'll put my hair up in a bun tomorrow night. That'll keep the headpiece from slipping."

"You don't need to wear the headpiece for rehearsal," Mrs. Sharp said.

"Yes, I do," Delight insisted. "Will you fix it?"

As Mrs. Sharp started to adjust the pins holding Delight's headpiece, Henry called, "Mrs. Sharp! The cassette player's busted! Want me to go to the media center and get another one?"

"Maybe it's just jammed." As she hurried over to the cassette player, Mrs. Sharp said to Delight, "Amber will fix your headpiece."

Amber stood rooted to the spot. Did Mrs. Sharp know what she was asking? Delight was Amber's enemy! She did *not* want to help her.

Delight's sandals scuffed the floorboards as she came over to the table. "Poke the pins in hard," she said, presenting her back to Amber. "You can't hurt me."

Amber gazed at the waterfall of honey-colored hair shimmering over turquoise-blue silk. It was such long, long hair. Because of Delight, Amber didn't have the longest hair in the class. Because of

Delight, Amber didn't have a best friend anymore. Because of Delight, Amber wasn't going to be the star in the Parents' Night program.

Delight had ruined Amber's third-grade year.

The scissors were still in her hand. Without realizing she was going to, Amber reached up and snipped off one side of Delight's hair, just below the earlobe.

The hank of golden hair swished to the floor. Both girls stared at the scattered silky threads as if the hair lying on the floor had nothing to do with them.

Then Delight screamed.

Chapter
NINE

At first Delight's scream was more of a shriek of surprise. Then, as she realized she was actually looking at her own hair lying on the floor, her scream became a high-pitched wail.

"What did you *do*?" she accused Amber. She reached up, feeling the short fringe of hair. Her eyes widened with disbelief.

"I didn't mean..." Amber stared at the hair on the floor, horrified. It wasn't true. She hadn't really cut off Delight's hair, had she?

"SHE CUT OFF MY HAIR!" Delight bellowed. "Mrs. Sharp! Amber cut off my hair!" Her wail now became sirenlike. The teacher came running over.

"What's going on here?" Then the teacher saw the sheaf of golden hair spilled on the floor and

Delight holding her hand over her ear as if she'd been wounded.

"Oh, my!" Mrs. Sharp drew in a shocked gasp. "Amber Gillian Cantrell! How could you do such an atrocious thing?"

Amber quaked inside. She didn't know what "atrocious" meant, but Mrs. Sharp was angrier than Amber had ever seen her. She had never used Amber's whole name before.

The scissors were still in her hand. There was no denying what she had done.

The whole class blasted Amber with accusations.

"I saw her!"

"Amber chopped off Delight's hair!"

"Amber did it! She's in trouble!"

Delight threw herself into her teacher's arms, sobbing as if her heart would break. "She cut my hair," she whimpered over and over. "Amber cut my hair!"

"Amber, go to the office right now," Mrs. Sharp ordered sternly. "When Mrs. Allan asks why you have been sent to her, tell her you cut off another child's hair. I'll be in to deal with you in a minute."

Ms. Lovejoy had dashed up on the stage when the commotion erupted. "How can I help?"

"I have to take this child to the nurse," Mrs. Sharp told her. "Would you watch my class?"

"Of course," Ms. Lovejoy replied.

Mrs. Sharp hurried out of the auditorium, her arm protectively around the still-sobbing Delight. Amber watched them, a cold, creeping sensation filling her stomach. She was in serious, serious trouble.

"Amber." Ms. Lovejoy went over to her and took the scissors from her lifeless fingers. "You'd better do what your teacher said."

She bent down and picked up the scattered golden hair. Then she put the silky strands into a plastic bag.

Amber wondered why her old teacher was saving Delight's hair. They couldn't put it back, could they?

The other kids milled around Amber suspiciously, as if they expected her to jump at them and slice their hair off, too. They whispered among themselves, flicking wary glances at her.

Across the stage, Mindy gawked open-mouthed at Amber. Then she turned away to murmur something to Carly and Lisa. Amber was sure Mindy hated her.

She looked up at Ms. Lovejoy, tears streaming down her cheeks. "I've really done it now, haven't I?" she said, hoping her old teacher didn't hate her, too.

Ms. Lovejoy sighed. "Yes, Amber. I'm afraid you have. Now, you'd better go to Mrs. Allan's office."

Mrs. Cantrell had to close the quilt store early to pick up Amber at school. Amber had never been sent home from school in her life.

Delight had already gone home. Amber had heard her sobbing all the way down the hall when Mrs. Wakefield came for her earlier.

The principal had asked Amber why she cut off Delight's hair. Amber did not have an answer, which made Mrs. Allan even madder. Then Mrs. Sharp came in and asked Amber the same question. Amber still did not have an answer. Both the principal and her teacher lectured her on the dangers of sharp scissors and told her what she had done was very, very wrong.

"Do you have anything to say for yourself?" Mrs. Allan asked Amber once more.

Amber shook her head. Her stomach hurt. She wanted to go home.

Now she squirmed in the "hot seat," the chair beside the secretary's desk, while her mother talked privately with the principal and Amber's teacher. No one in the office spoke to her. Amber figured they were avoiding her because they knew she had done something horrible.

At last her mother came out of Mrs. Allan's office. "Let's go home," was all her mother said.

In the car Amber fastened her seat belt without having to be told. "Did Mrs. Allan throw me out of school?" she asked fearfully. As much as she disliked third grade, she didn't want to be expelled.

"No," her mother replied. "Let's wait until we get home to discuss this."

They rode home in tense silence. Amber's thoughts were a jumble of all the awful things that could happen to her as a result of chopping off Delight's hair. They would make Amber sit in the time-out desk the rest of the year. They would make her do extra homework every single night. Or, she thought with icy dread, they would cut off *her* hair. And they would let Delight hold the scissors.

Carriage Street was deserted. Inside, their house had a dusty midday stillness. Justin was still at school. Amber felt strange, coming home in the middle of the day.

"I'm going to make some hot chocolate," Mrs. Cantrell said, going into the kitchen.

Amber sat down at the table in her usual place. Her heart pounded. What was her mother going to say? When her mother set a steaming mug of cocoa in front of her, Amber glanced up anxiously.

Mrs. Cantrell sat down opposite her. "Your teacher and Mrs. Allan said you couldn't tell them why you did such a terrible thing. Can you tell me?"

"No," Amber replied quaveringly. "I didn't mean to cut her hair off. It just sort of...happened."

Her mother frowned. "Amber, that's not good enough. It didn't just 'happen.' You had the scissors in your hand. You deliberately cut off another child's hair. What happened between you and that girl? She's Mindy's new friend, isn't she?"

Amber nodded miserably. "Mom," she said, starting to cry, "I'm having an awful year!"

Her mother softened a bit. "I know. I know you and Mindy aren't getting along. I know you don't like Delight. And I know you're not overly fond of your teacher this year."

"She's not like Ms. Lovejoy."

"Of course she isn't. Mrs. Sharp is a different person. Everyone can't be like Ms. Lovejoy. Some teachers you will like, some you won't. Besides, I think Mrs. Sharp has been fair. She let you go back to Ms. Lovejoy's class that time."

Amber wiped her tears with the back of her hand. "You heard about that?"

"Your teacher told me a lot of things about you today. The point is that you have to learn to get along with people, Amber. That's what life is all about."

Her mother's words sounded familiar. Just the other day, in social studies, Mrs. Sharp had told the class the very same thing, that people have to learn to get along with each other, whether they are friends or not.

"I think I know why you cut Delight Wakefield's hair," her mother said suddenly.

"You do?" Amber looked at her in surprise. How

did her mother know something Amber herself didn't know?

"Yes. I did something like that myself, once."

Amber took a sip of her cocoa, eager to hear her mother's story.

"When I was your age," Mrs. Cantrell began, "I went to school with a girl named Nadine Vasquez. Nadine was an only child. She had two horses. She went to Florida during the Christmas holidays. Everybody wanted to be Nadine's friend."

"Were you her friend?" Amber asked.

"No. I couldn't stand Nadine Vasquez." Her mother said the name as if she still couldn't stand Nadine Vasquez after all these years. Amber was stunned. Her mother had just told her to try to get along with people and now she admitted she couldn't stand this girl!

"I was jealous of Nadine," Mrs. Cantrell explained. "Nadine had everything I didn't have. She was pretty, popular..."

"Did she have long hair?"

"No. But she used to wear white boots to school." Her mother smiled, remembering. "This was back when go-go boots were all the rage. Nadine was the only kid in elementary school who had a pair. They were white leather and they came from London. Her father brought them back from a business trip."

Amber wondered if her mother had done

something awful to Nadine's boots.

Mrs. Cantrell continued her story. "One day we had tumbling in gym class. We all had to take off our shoes. Nadine took her boots off and put them by her desk. The rest of the class left for the gym, but I lagged behind. I saw Nadine's cartridge pen on her desk. Cartridge ink pens were another fad that year. I picked up her pen and scratched her white leather boots. Later, I found out the ink in Nadine's pen was permanent. The marks would never come off. Her expensive boots were ruined."

Amber had no idea her mother had ever done anything bad. "What happened?"

"Well, I confessed I was the guilty one. I thought I would have to pay for the boots. I was terrified because I imagined they cost thousands of dollars and I was afraid my parents wouldn't have the money and I'd be sent to jail. It was very confusing because although I was scared to death, secretly I was glad Nadine couldn't wear those boots anymore. You see, I wasn't having a very good year either, and I blamed Nadine. I was jealous of her. That's why I ruined her boots."

Amber was quiet. She realized she was jealous of Delight Wakefield. She had been jealous of her since the very first day of school, when she had looked across the room and saw the girl with hair she could sit on.

Her mother studied her thoughtfully. "I think you blame Delight Wakefield for the things that have happened to you this year. Out of frustration and jealousy, you cut off Delight's hair. Am I right?"

"I guess so." Amber wished she could blink herself back in the auditorium, like that pretty genie on the old television show. If she had to live that moment over, she would put down the scissors and fix Delight's headpiece like Mrs. Sharp had asked her to.

Her mother's tone became stern. "Just because I understand why you cut off Delight's hair doesn't mean I excuse such behavior for a second. I ought to ground you, but I think you need to work this problem out with Mindy. So I'm cutting off TV until the end of this report card period."

Amber waited, knowing her mother was not finished.

"I will speak to Delight's mother. But you have to do what my parents made me do when I ruined Nadine Vasquez's boots."

"What was that?" Amber was afraid of the answer.

"Apologize to Delight," Mrs. Cantrell said firmly. "You can't just say you're sorry, either. Saying you're sorry won't automatically wipe out what you did."

"What do you mean?"

"You have to apologize to Delight in a special way, so she knows you mean it. And Amber," her mother added, "you have to mean it. That will be the hard part."

"How can I apologize to her? She hates me!" Amber wished she could just write sentences: *I will not cut Delight's hair* a hundred times. Even a million times.

"You'll have to figure that out for yourself." Her mother got up to rinse the mugs. "You won't feel good about yourself until you do."

Then she went to call Delight's mother. She made the call from the phone in her sewing room, with the door closed.

Amber went into her own room. She curled up on her bed and hugged R.C.

"You're the only friend I have left," she whispered. The raccoon smiled its bland, stitched smile.

Her mother was in the sewing room a long time. When she came out, she opened Amber's door.

"Mrs. Wakefield was very upset," she reported. "They just got back from Hair Magic at the mall."

"How is Delight?" Amber asked in a small voice.

"She's upset, too. Her hair is ruined." Her mother sighed.

"Will Delight still be the star in the program tomorrow night?"

"I don't know anything about tomorrow night," her mother said. "Was Delight the star?"

"Yes," Amber replied, burying her face in her

raccoon's soft fur. "That's why Daddy isn't coming. Because Delight is the star. Not me."

Her mother came over to her bed and sat down. "Is that what you think? That your father doesn't want to see you in the play unless you're the star?"

"I was the star last year, he keeps telling me. I know he wanted me to be the star this year, too," Amber said miserably. "And I'm not, so he's not coming."

Mrs. Cantrell folded Amber into her arms. "Oh, honey. You don't have to be the star. Your father loves you very much, you know."

"But we hardly see him anymore." A tear dripped onto R.C.'s ear.

Her mother held her close. "It hasn't been easy for you and Justin. But it hasn't been easy for your father, either. He feels like he's no longer part of the family. And his job has made it even more difficult. Amber, you don't have to prove to your father that you're good enough for him to come see you. He thinks you and Justin are the greatest kids in the world. And so do I."

Amber cried into her mother's shoulder. "Even now?"

Her mother kissed the top of her head. "I don't always like the things you *do*, but I love who you are. You're my daughter."

They sat that way, with the raccoon squashed

between them, until Amber stopped crying.

The next day, Amber walked hesitantly into Room Six.

Spotting her, Henry exclaimed, "Here comes the hair-slasher! Hey, Amber, how come you didn't cut off your own hair while you were at it?"

Mrs. Sharp fixed him with her famous look. "There is no call for that, Henry. What happened yesterday is none of your concern." Then she got out her roll book and began to take attendance.

Delight, Amber noticed, was absent.

"Take out your social studies books and turn to page twenty-five," Mrs. Sharp said.

Amber took out her book gratefully. For once, she was glad Mrs. Sharp stuck to a routine.

Mindy kept sneaking uneasy glances at Amber, as if she were sitting next to a dangerous animal. Amber wished Mindy would say something to her, *anything* to break the awful silence between them.

At lunch, Lisa was the only one who would eat with Amber. "Why did you do it?" she asked bluntly.

Amber knew Mindy, sitting at the other end with Carly, had heard the question and was waiting for Amber's answer. "It's complicated," she said lamely. She couldn't admit she had cut off Delight's hair because she was jealous.

"Do you think she'll ever come back?" Lisa

wanted to know.

Amber wasn't sure. Delight must feel pretty bad to stay out of school. She hadn't missed a day yet.

That evening was Parents' Night. Amber's class performed their Other Lands parade in the assembly. Amber circled the stage in a trance, barely remembering to say, "I'm Turkey." She glimpsed her father in the audience. He had made it after all.

They were going out for pizza later, just the two of them. Next week he was taking Justin to a ball game. "If I have to miss a weekend," her father promised her, "I will see you during the week." For the first time, Amber's stomach did not twinge.

But Delight was not there. No one wore the beautiful turquoise Japanese costume.

On Friday, Delight came back to school. Amber gasped when she saw her enter the room.

Delight now had short hair, as short as Mindy's. Her honey-colored hair framed her pale face in feathery layers.

She went directly to her seat like a tin soldier, without speaking to anyone. She even ignored Carly when her friend ran over to admire her new hair style.

Delight bent her head over her work, as if ashamed to be seen without her long, beautiful hair. Her neck looked different, like the neck of a baby duck, Amber thought.

Now Amber had the longest hair in class. It still wasn't long enough to sit on, but no one else had hair as long as Amber's.

She wondered why she didn't feel good about that.

Chapter
TEN

Before she knocked on Mr. Laidlaw's door, Amber poised her pen professionally over her clipboard. Some people didn't want to be pestered by kids on a Saturday morning, so she was determined to look businesslike.

She knocked on the door. Mr. Laidlaw was the last person Amber had to interview for her social studies project. He was the Secret Service agent. She was glad she had saved the best for last.

Across the street from the Laidlaw house, Amber saw Mindy interviewing Mr. Potts, the septic tank man. Mr. Potts was washing his car with his children. There was a lot of splashing and squealing. Mindy was doubled over, laughing. Amber could tell she was having a good time.

Mrs. Laidlaw answered the door. When Amber

told her she wanted to speak to her husband, Mrs. Laidlaw directed Amber to the side of the house, where he was fixing the gutter.

She walked around to the side yard and found the Secret Service agent clinging to a ladder that was leaning against the roof. He didn't look very interviewable, but Amber launched ahead anyway.

"Mr. Laidlaw?" she called. "I'm Amber Cantrell from down the street. I was wondering if I could talk to you about your job. It's for school. We're supposed to interview people in our neighborhood."

"Fire away," he said, hammering nails into the gutter.

"Can you tell me about your job?"

He drove a nail in, then replied. "I work for the Secret Service. It's a branch of the Treasury Department. A lot of people don't realize that. They think we're part of the FBI. The Secret Service was originally formed back in the 1860s to track down counterfeit money, but when President McKinley was assassinated, the Secret Service became guards for the President and his family."

Amber wrote swiftly, not even trying to spell words like "counterfeit" and "assassinate." "But what do *you* do?" she pressed.

"Oh, I follow the President around. Ow!" He mashed his thumb with the hammer. "Wherever the President goes, I go."

"Is it exciting, being with the President?" she asked.

"Sometimes." He was concentrating on straightening the bent gutter.

Amber glanced over her shoulder at Mindy. She and Mr. Potts' children were throwing soapy sponges at each other. Mindy's interview was going a lot better than Amber's.

"What do you do for fun?" she asked, deciding she had enough information on the "work" side of her interview sheet.

"Fix up the house." He grinned down at her. "Just kidding. My wife and I play golf."

Golf was even more boring than fixing the house, Amber thought. What was fun about hitting a little white ball into a hole in the ground?

"Well, I think I have enough," she said. "Thanks, Mr. Laidlaw."

She left, disappointed that her Secret Service agent had turned out to be so dull. If she and Mindy had done their project together, they would have giggled over Mr. Laidlaw's "exciting" job.

At home, Amber sat on the stoop. She wished she had someone to play with.

It was still pretty early. Mrs. Cantrell had recently hired a college student to work in the shop on Saturdays. She wasn't going to the store until Amber's father came to take Amber and Justin to the movies. But that wouldn't be until after lunch. In the meantime, Amber had nothing to do.

The morning was brisk and windy, ideal for making a kite for R.C. But making things wasn't as fun without someone else to share it with, she had discovered. She could start writing her neighborhood report, but she didn't feel like it.

She stuck her hands in her pockets and felt two round disks. The "R.C. and P." buttons. She had put them in her pocket this morning. What a joke, a secret club with no members.

She got up and wandered down Carriage Street. There was a clean car in front of Mr. Potts' house, but that was all. Mr. Potts and his kids were probably inside. Mindy must have gone home.

Amber walked all the way to the bridge over Rocky Run. A lone figure stood at the rail, watching the muddy water. The curve of the girl's back looked sad. Short, feathery hair blew about in the wind.

It was Delight Wakefield.

Amber watched Delight for a few minutes. She looked even lonelier than Amber felt. Her mind flashed back to that awful day in the auditorium, when Delight scuffed over to have Amber fix her headpiece. "Stick the pins in hard," Delight had instructed. "You can't hurt me."

But she had.

She had done a terrible, terrible thing, cut off

another person's hair because her own hair wasn't as pretty. If Delight hated her for the rest of her life, Amber wouldn't blame her.

If only she could apologize. She *was* sorry, truly she was. How could she ever make it up to Delight?

For an instant, Amber considered cutting off her own hair. She could do it right in front of Delight, just take the scissors and slice off her own ponytail. She would even hand Delight her chopped-off hair. But that wouldn't make Delight feel better. Delight buried her face in her hands. Amber knew she was crying.

Then Amber thought of the perfect apology. She would give Delight the thing that meant more to her than anything on earth.

She would give her R.C.

Racing back home, Amber ran into her bedroom and snatched the raccoon off her bed. She sprinted down the street with a stitch stabbing her side, hoping Delight was still on the bridge.

She was.

Shyly, Amber approached the other girl, the raccoon hidden behind her back.

"Hi," she said.

Delight looked up, startled. "Oh," she said flatly. "It's you." She scrubbed at her cheek with the heel of her hand, then turned, as if to leave.

"Please don't run away," Amber said. "I know you

hate me and I don't blame you. Here." She thrust R.C. into Delight's arms.

She felt a pang as she gave Delight her beloved stuffed animal. She hadn't felt the magic of last summer in a long time, not since she and Mindy had their fight. But it was still hard to give away her only friend in the world.

"Your raccoon," Delight said, puzzled.

"She's yours now." Amber rattled off her speech before she lost her nerve. "She comes with her own newspaper and magazines and clothes. Mindy has Pearl, her best friend. Since Mindy's your best friend now, it all works out. R.C. is a really good friend. I want you to have her. I know it doesn't give you your long hair back, but, um…it's all I have. I hope it makes you feel better."

Delight held the raccoon out as if it had germs. "I don't know if I want anything from you, Amber Gillian Cantrell."

Amber wished people would stop using her whole name. It didn't sound so wonderful anymore. "Please," she begged. "I know how you feel…"

"No, you don't," Delight said sharply. "Nobody cut off *your* hair."

Amber swallowed. This was true. "It's all I have to give you," she repeated weakly.

"You know, when I first came here, I wanted to be your friend," Delight confided. "But then I found out you were stuck up."

"Me!" Amber pointed unbelievingly to herself. "*You* thought *I* was stuck up!"

"Yeah. You were always whispering to Mindy. And you have that secret club…"

"Had. Mindy quit. She gave me her button. I guess you guys can have the buttons and you can start the club again. Without me in it."

Delight looked away. "I used to watch you and Mindy in school. You guys always seemed to have such a good time together. I never had a best friend—we moved around too much."

"You do now," Amber argued. "You've got Mindy!"

Delight swung her gaze back to Amber. "Do you think I took Mindy from you?"

"She's not my best friend anymore. She's your best friend."

Delight shook her head. "Mindy talks about you all the time. She says you have lots of neat ideas. She told me she wished she could think up ideas like you do."

Amber felt a jab of guilt. She thought Mindy was getting tired of her ideas and that was why she was more interested in Delight. But maybe Mindy would like them to use one of her ideas sometime. Getting along with people, Amber realized, meant letting them have a turn.

"Everybody likes you," she said to Delight. "You have more friends than anybody I know."

"They like me because I'm nice to them. If you're extra nice when you go to a new place, people like you. My parents promised when we moved to Virginia that we'd stay here a long time," Delight said. "No more moving around. At first I was glad. Now I don't know. I wish we *would* move again."

Suddenly she thrust the stuffed raccoon back at Amber. "I can't take it."

A lump rose in Amber's throat. Delight was giving back the one thing Amber truly loved. How could Amber ever apologize to her now?

"I'm sorry," she whispered, even though her mother said the words alone would do no good. "I'm really sorry." Then she added honestly, "I hope you don't move. Not on account of...you know."

"I felt awful when the lady cut off the rest of my hair," Delight admitted. "I mean, I've had long hair all my life! I didn't know who I was. Every time I looked in the mirror I thought it was somebody else."

Amber nodded. "I felt sort of like that when my father left. I wasn't sure what was happening for a long time." She realized that she and Delight had something in common. They were both uncertain at times—Delight because she was always moving to a new place, Amber because she was still adjusting to her parents' divorce.

"My father says I look cute with short hair," Delight said. "Before, you couldn't see my face."

"You do have a nice face," Amber said.

Delight smiled and tweaked one of R.C.'s ears. "Nobody ever gave me anything so special before. She wouldn't be happy with me. Why make her move? Besides, Row-Bear would be jealous."

Amber felt a smile spread across her own face. Was Delight accepting her apology? She hugged R.C. "Row-Bear is cool. Why don't you bring him over to my house sometime? We could make them kites. A raccoon kite for R.C. and a doggy kite for Row-Bear."

"Then I can be in your club? I've wanted to join ever since the first day of school."

"You have your own club," Amber reminded her.

"My club is kind of boring."

"But the whole class is in it," Amber said. "Everybody wants to be your friend."

"But nobody wants to be my *best* friend." Delight scraped her sneaker over the bottom rail of the bridge.

Amber remembered what Mindy had said on Trade Day a few weeks ago. Maybe three friends *would* work out just fine. In fact, three was a better number than two.

"We'll start a new club. Only best friends allowed," Amber said. "I mean, if you still want to..."

Delight's answering smile told Amber she had

given her the best gift of all.

"Hey," Delight cried. "Here comes Mindy."

Amber watched her ex-best friend cross the bridge. "Hi," she said.

Mindy looked at them. "I saw you guys up here. What's going on?"

Amber wasn't sure what to say. Was Mindy mad at her for talking to Delight?

"We were talking about the club," Delight told her. "Amber wants to start a new one."

Mindy glanced at Amber. "A new club? With all of us? Good. At least it'll be something to do."

Amber knew this was Mindy's way of saying she wanted to be friends again. She pulled the button out of her pocket and handed it to Mindy. Then she passed her own button to Delight. "I'll get another one made, since there are three of us in the club now," she said. "Should we change the initials? R.B. for Row-Bear should be on it, too."

"No," Delight said, pinning the button to her shirt. "It's okay."

Mindy grinned at Amber. "If we're all going to be in the club, you ought to get your hair cut short."

"Yeah," Delight giggled. "So you'll look like us!"

Amber laughed too, but she wasn't about to give up her long hair. Not when it was almost long enough to sit on.

"Why don't we go to my house and have a club

meeting?" Mindy suggested.

"Good idea," Amber said.

A car rolled up on the bridge.

"Amber," Mrs. Cantrell called out the window. "I'm going to the grocery store. Justin is back at the house. Do you want to come with me?"

"No, Mindy and Delight and me are going over to Mindy's house," she called back.

"Mindy and Delight and *I*," her mother corrected before pulling off again.

"You said it!" Amber agreed happily.

As the three of them crossed over the bridge, Amber noticed the beavers had rebuilt their dam. It looked stronger than before.

She gave her raccoon a squeeze and thought she saw R.C. wink back at her. Was it a trick of the light?

It could have been magic, Amber decided, walking down Carriage Street with her two friends.

Anything was possible.